The Purging Fire

THE PURGING FIRE

4 Elements of Mystery Book 1

Marlene Mesot

Print layout and e-book conversion by
DLD Books Editing and Self-Publishing Services
www.dldbooks.com

Unless otherwise noted, all scripture references are from the New American Standard Bible, Giant Print Edition, Thomas Nelson Publishers, The Lockman Foundation, LaHabra CA, ©1977.

2nd Edition

© 2018 by Marlene Mesot

All rights reserved.

ISBN: 979-8-9858477-6-5

4 Elements of Mystery Series

1. The Purging Fire
2. The Snowball Effect
3. Whirlwind of Fear
4. Terra Terror

More Mysteries

The Cat Stalker's Sonnets

www.marlsmenagerie.com

2 Corinthians 12:10

Therefore, I am well content with weakness, with insults, with distresses, with persecutions, with difficulties, for Christ's sake, for when I am weak then I am strong.

Acknowledgments

First, I wish to thank my best friend since early childhood, Jeanne Petrin, for her prayers and constant support. I will treasure her always.

I would also like to thank her husband, Bob, for some advice and resources when I was writing my first novel, *The Purging Fire*. Robert Petrin worked approximately twenty-four years for the Concord Fire Department, Concord, New Hampshire, finishing there as a battalion chief. When he left there, he became a fire chief in East Derry New Hampshire, where he retired from fire service. He taught fire courses at the New Hampshire Technical College for about seven years. He left there and is teaching through the Fire Academy. He goes to different fire stations throughout the state.

I also thank Jeanne for this information.

Contents

1 Alarming Events 13
2 Desperate Dreams 21
3 Meaningful Meetings 27
5 Old Maid 43
6 Smoke Rises 53
7 As the Smoke Thickens 63
8 Winter's Loving Chill 71
9 Approaching Judgment 81
10 The Final Test 89
11 All Things New 103
12 Be My Valentine 119
13 A Spark of Reality 135
14 Running Scared 165
15 The Burning Pain 173
16 Tandemonium 183
17 The Heart of the Matter 189
18 The Purging Fire 197
19 Art Smart 203
20 A Future Inkling 209

A sneak peek at the next novel, *The Snowball Effect.*

4 Blind Fear..221

Bonus Material

Where Will You Turn?..233
    Act 1, Scene 1..235
    Act I, Scene 2..237
    Act I, Scene 3..239
    Act I, Scene 4...243

About the Author..245

1

Alarming Events

Melissa squealed as the alarm blared its urgent warning. Instantly, her hands covered her ears to turn off her hearing aids. The alarm's persistent buzzing continued to penetrate the abrupt silence even though her amplifiers now served as earplugs.

Someone was pulling at her left elbow and leading Melissa toward the door of the student bookstore. She saw other people moving quickly in the same direction. Melissa turned her head to be able to see her guide on her blind side. She recognized the burnt-orange sweater and shoulder-length, golden-blond hair of her freshman roommate Zoe Babette.

A crowd was gathering behind the Student Union Building on the lawn of the Iandale State College campus. Melissa Sanders turned her hearing aids back on to catch the words of her roommate's clear, low-pitched voice.

". . . Be another bomb threat!" Zoe exclaimed. "The fire alarms are getting a workout this year, huh?"

Melissa nodded. The background noise of murmuring voices made it difficult to distinguish one from the muffle.

"Missy, Zoe, hi." Melissa's friend Laurie Gibbs was nudging

her way through the crowd toward them. "What a scare." Laurie passed her hand over her forehead and then pushed her long, brown hair back over her shoulders.

When she reached her friends, Laurie continued to explain, "I had to lock the bookstore cashbox before I could leave. I'm glad I don't work in the coffee shop down the other end of the building. You know how big that place is."

"Oh my, yes," Melissa agreed. "The building is used by the Iandale residents too. How many of the faculty is here now? Zoe, isn't that Dr. Francis, our creative writing teacher, over there? I recognize her heavy gray sweater."

"That's heavy blue sweater," Zoe corrected and grinned.

"Whatever," Melissa agreed, "but it looks gray from here."

"Hey, Laurie, is that her husband she's clinging to?"

"Uh-huh, Zoe. You don't see much of him around here."

"What does he look like?" Missy asked.

Zoe laughed and then answered, "He looks like a man." After a moment, she began to describe the man in question, Todd Francis. "He's tall. Dr. Francis barely reaches his chin when she is standing straight. He has dark-brown, I'd say bushy hair and a full brown beard to match. He is wearing one of those London Fog raincoats."

"Todd, I wish those fire marshals would hurry up and decide what is going on," Barbara Francis complained to her husband. She leaned her head against his chest, crushing her tight golden-blond curls.

"Be patient, love. Give them time."

"I knew it was going to be a bad day this morning when I got up with a migraine."

The flashing and single cry of a fire truck's siren captured everyone's attention. It stopped abruptly in front of the Student Union building on Center Street.

"Oh my goodness, is there a fire this time?" Melissa spoke in a high whisper. Under her burgundy turtleneck, she shivered.

"Sh, sh, sh, here comes one of the fire marshals now," Zoe told her. "It's the cute blond guy that you like from your Christian group. The leader, there, what's his name?"

"Oh, you mean Alexander Marcus, the leader?" Then she named the group. "Yeah, he's cute. I like blonds." Melissa's face felt hot.

"Okay, folks. Attention please." Although his voice sounded soothing and pleasant, Alex Marcus spoke with authority.

Missy stood on tiptoe to try to distinguish the tall, muscular frame of Alexander Marcus from the rest of the group. She adjusted the volume control on her left hearing aid, instantly alert to hear what he was saying. Inwardly, she scolded herself as she felt the heavy thudding of her own heartbeat.

"We are going to have to close the Student Union for a couple of hours to clean up," Alex was explaining. He spoke in a loud clear voice. He paused in his speech when he saw his roommate, Arthur Wills, emerge from the building and approach.

Arthur Wills, although slimmer, topped Alex's nearly six-foot height by another four inches. In contrast, Arthur had coal-black hair and black eyes that were accented by his gray, short-sleeved shirt and black Levis.

"What's happening, Zo?" Melissa asked impatiently.

"Huh? Oh, I was just thinking how different they look, Alex and Arthur. They're both standing side by side by the door."

"I see you didn't forget Art's name," Melissa teased. "What is Alex wearing? I mean, what color clothes?"

"Yeah." Zoe poked at Melissa's arm playfully. "He is wearing a light-blue pinstriped shirt and dark blue Wranglers. Hmm. Alex looks nice in blue, Missy, it matches his eyes."

Arthur cleared his throat to speak in his deep, nasal-sounding voice. "It seems, people, there has been a small fire in the bookstore basement. Most of the books that came in for next semester recently will have to be replaced, I'm afraid."

Art's coal-black eyes focused on Melissa's friend, Laurie Gibbs, who was standing near him in the front of the crowd.

"More work for you, Laurie."

With a jerk of his head, Arthur shot a glance in the direction of a shorter redheaded young man. Peter Early, a senior at Iandale State College, was editor in chief of the college newspaper, the *Iandale Inkling*.

Again Arthur's directness was obvious to those around him.

"Don't worry, Pete. You'll get your scoop." Then Arthur made a dismissing gesture with a wave of his hand and walked away.

"We'll be investigating the cause," Alex added.

"Oh boy, another mess to clean up," Joe Burns, the college handyman, snarled. "Always something. Probably a college prankster."

Melissa and Zoe turned as they heard Joe's gruff voice muttering behind them.

"Gee, Mr. Burns, you didn't have anything else to do today, did you?" Melissa attempted to tease the elder man.

"Oh, ya, that's what you think, young lady? And my boss, Mr. McGuire, is always complainin' that I work too slow anyway. And why don't I just retire because I'm old enough. He keeps remindin' me."

"Don't let people bug ya, Mr. Burns," Melissa encouraged. "Whatever you do, do your work heartily as for the Lord and not for men." Melissa quoted from Colossians 3:23. "If you know you are doing your best, I don't think you should let someone else's opinion discourage you."

"What does God care whether I trim the hedges evenly or not?" Joe Burns snapped. "You young kids don't know what you're talking about half the time. I gotta go. I have work to do."

"Boy, he surely doesn't like to be preached to."

"You have to know how to take him, Zoe," Melissa said. "I wasn't trying to preach. I was trying to encourage the man."

"Aha." Zoe nodded her head in disbelief. "I've got to be going, Missy. It's time for my last class. I'll meet you at the dining commons for supper, all right?"

"Yeah, Zo, see you later."

Missy sighed as she approached the left-hand line outside the dining hall later that day. It was the shorter of the two. Once inside, students filed past stacks of trays, which were located in the middle, between the two lines. The overhead menu, which Missy couldn't see to read as it was too high and too far away for her close vision, was posted above the serving area. Students slid their trays along a cafeteria-style line, to the left and to the right, which opened into two separate larger rooms with tables and chairs and a common drink area for milk and hot water in the center. Missy hesitated as she approached the block of trays, trying to see. The menu was written in white on a blackboard, but the print was too small.

Then Missy heard a male voice bark impatiently behind her.

"Keep it moving! Hurry up!"

She turned to see a young man with brown hair standing behind her slide a tray off the rack. She turned back, stepped to the metal bars, placed her tray down, and *guessed* at the choices as she slid her tray along. She was too shy to ask strangers for help.

After getting her hot tea water, Missy walked to a table by

the window at the back of a still-empty row. She was picking at her plate when a male voice spoke beside her. This voice was soothing, unlike the rude guy behind her in the serving line.

"Hi, Missy. May I join you?"

She looked up to see a handsome tall blond man standing beside her. Her heart had seemingly joined the food in her mouth, so she nodded. She looked down at her plate. Her heart began to pound as he sat directly across from her. She looked up tentatively.

He asked, "Do you mind if my roommate Art joins us? He should be coming along soon."

"No, that's fine. My roommate Zoe will be here as well, and maybe my friend Laurie from the bookstore." She picked at her plate for a few seconds then ventured to ask, "Alex, could you tell me what this stuff is. I couldn't tell."

He smiled. Then he told her, "You have sliced turkey in front of you, peas, and mashed potato. On your tray you have peaches at the top-left side and butterscotch pudding on the right."

"Thank you," she replied.

Again he smiled and then responded. "Anytime, my pleasure."

They ate in companionable silence until their roommates joined them.

Once settled, Art took a packet from his pocket and shook the contents into his cup of hot water.

When Zoe asked what he was doing, he replied, "Decaf. The stuff they serve here doesn't qualify as even instant coffee."

Missy added, "Zoe likes her herbal tea as well."

Alex said, "I guess we all have our eccentricities," as he picked up his teacup.

Another girl joined them. "Sorry I'm late. I had to help close the bookstore after we took stock of everything. What a mess."

Alex asked, "Was there much damage, Laurie?"

"Fortunately not a huge loss. Some of the textbooks for next semester will have to be reordered. We lost a few supplies, but the fire was contained quickly. Thanks to our brave fire marshals here."

"Just doing our job," Arthur said quickly. He sawed at his turkey with fork and knife.

"Hi, gang. Have you heard the latest news?"

Peter Early was pulling a chair from a nearby table over to join the group.

Art sniffed and then commented, "If you mean the bookstore fire, you're a bit late. We were all there. Remember?"

Pete shook his head. "No, I mean about the mental patient who escaped from the state hospital in Concord earlier today. At last report, he was said to be heading west."

Heads came up.

Zoe was the first to speak. "You mean, he might be headed this way?"

Pete nodded.

Alex said, "No, we hadn't heard about that."

"Yeah," Pete continued, "there's a statewide manhunt out looking for him by now."

Pete pointed to Art's tray. "Somebody likes pudding." Art had taken two dishes for himself.

"I like butterscotch," Art replied then scooped some potato into his mouth.

Missy spoke, "I can agree with that."

They ate in silence for a time.

Finally, Zoe asked, "So, Pete, how did you get to become editor of the town paper at such a young age?"

Pete grinned. "Thanks. I worked with my uncle at the paper

since I was in high school, and he recently retired and gave it to my charge. He also suggested I come back to school to complete my journalism degree, so here I am. Fortunately, it's almost there since this is my senior year."

Alex teased, "Scoop 'em, Pete."

2

Desperate Dreams

"He is really a nice guy," Missy told her roommate when she returned to her dorm that evening. Her inner joy glowed through her smile.

"I thought you liked him," Zoe smiled too.

"No, I mean as a person," Missy protested. "He really cares about people, and he's a natural leader the way he takes charge in a situation. I respect his Christian role model."

"Yeah, sure," Zoe retorted. Zoe continued to brush out her golden curls. They sprang back exuberantly when they were pulled down past her shoulder. She was sitting on her bed, wearing her favorite beige night gown and yellow-and-brown robe.

Melissa, by now, had traded her burgundy turtleneck and blue jeans for her yellow flannel night gown and yellow robe. She came over to Zoe's bed, looking for her slippers. She bent down to feel along the wall that separated the beds from the parallel bureaus. Their desks were on the other side of the U-shaped room, where they were backed up against the middle bureau and closet section. The other outside wall of the U, opposite the beds, contained a coat rack and several chairs by it. In her search, Melissa found Zoe's brown slippers, which had a small plastic bumblebee attached to each foot. Next to them she felt a soft artificial fur material and saw the plain-yellow pair that belonged to her.

"Here are my foot warmers." As she stood up, Melissa could see her new friend more closely.

She could see the gold chain of Zoe's necklace hanging outside her night clothes. "Don't you take that off, Zo?"

"Ha?" Missy's voice had interrupted her thoughts.

"Your necklace. Don't you take it off when you go to bed?"

"No. I wear it almost all the time. I guess it's sort of a keepsake. It was supposed to have been given to me by my mother. You remember, I told you that I am an orphan and I never knew my parents?"

Missy nodded. "Can I ask you what's in it?"

"Yeah, sure." Zoe slipped the gold chain from around her neck and handed it to her friend.

The object hanging from the chain was oval shaped and dark brown in color with raised crisscrossing lines running around it in a slanted pattern. As Missy felt its hard clay texture, the depth of the round clay object impressed her. It was about an inch in diameter.

Zoe took it from Missy, opened it, then handed it back for closer inspection.

"Can you see the tiny plastic queen bee inside, Missy? Bees fascinate me."

"Oh, so it's a beehive."

"Yeah. I put the queen bee inside. I didn't have any other photos to use."

"That is unique." Missy handed it back.

After a moment of thought, she asked, "Zo, why are you majoring in English literature and not biology?"

"Because, counselor, I can study bees on my own. Science isn't my thing. Besides, someday I want to be a journalist. That is, provided I don't become a bee keeper first."

They both laughed.

"Well, I'm getting sleepy."

Missy got up to go to her own bed. She stretched and then got under her covers.

Zoe too climbed under her blankets to sleep.

"Good night, Missy."

In her dream, Zoe Babette again found herself running through a long corridor with many doorways on either side. Her breath thudded in her chest, and her lungs ached. Each breath came harder. Zoe grabbed at the doorknobs as she passed, but each one seemed to be locked. She looked back to see shadowy figures moving behind her. She tried to quicken her pace, but the corridor seemed endless. The beige-colored walls, chocolate-brown doors, and brown-and-white patchwork carpeting of the long hallway were all ingrained in her mind now as the dream continued to repeat itself over and over again, growing more frequent with the years.

Zoe screamed as a baby's wailing suddenly shattered the silence.

"Where are you?" Zoe yelled urgently. "Where are you?"

Abruptly, to her left, a staircase appeared. Automatically Zoe stopped running and stood frozen to the spot. Her throat was dry, and her head began to throb as she stood motionless.

Oh, no, she thought to herself, *not again. No, I won't go down there.*

It was the same spiral staircase with the patchwork carpeting and wrought iron railing that she had seen countless times before. It wound down and around into a high ceiling entranceway with individual pictures of unknown people on the ivory-colored walls. A seven-foot-high circle arch about four feet long distinctly marked the entranceway leading to an ivory-colored steel door with no window. A large oriental rug, a mixture of brown and deep-rose color, hid the floor.

As Zoe stood looking down into the vast emptiness of the lower room, she could see out of the corner of her eye that the movements of the shadowy figures had quickened. The shapeless dark forms had seemed to increase in number too. Undistinguishable whispers began to mingle with the wailing baby's cries.

"Stop it. Stop it!"

Zoe's screams were not heeded.

As she reached out to grasp the railing, her hand seemed to stick to it. Her hand refused to slide easily when she began to descend the wide steps. She tried to run but couldn't. Each step seemed to be going in slow motion, and the staircase wound down and down endlessly.

Abruptly, Zoe found herself standing in one corner of a large kitchen. On the stove to her right, a pot of water boiled briskly, but she saw no one. On the counter next to the stove, a stack of white bath towels sat waiting . . .

"Do what you must do."

Zoe screamed heartily.

Above the dark-brown oak table floated the figure of an elderly woman. Her lined and wrinkled face contorted as she repeated the phrase. "Do what you must do." Her snow-white hair hugged her head in tight pin curls, and she wore a deep rose-colored robe.

Zoe stood motionless, screaming and yet staring at the woman while the apparition smiled down at her, repeating its only phrase.

Someone was calling her name. No one had ever called to Zoe before in this dream . . .

With a start, Zoe bolted up right in bed, forcing her eyes to open. Instinctively, Zoe clung to Melissa with grateful sobs of relief.

The fire alarm blurted its message without warning.

Both girls screamed and jumped. Zoe threw off her blankets and stood to scramble into her slippers.

Melissa, although not wearing hearing aids, still covered her ears.

"Where are my slippers?" she yelled.

Zoe pointed to her feet, which were surrounded by the yellow furry slippers. Zoe grasped her arm and led her out the door of their corner room, down the two flights of stairs to the lobby, and out of the building.

"Nice chilly night for a bomb scare." Laurie Gibbs and her roommate Susan joined them outside on the front walkway.

"We were both having nightmares when that stupid alarm bellowed," Melissa told her.

Laurie and Sue roomed on the same floor as Zoe and Melissa.

"They must be trying to teach us to fly like falcons. We seem to have a drill at the drop of a hat—I mean, bomb." Susan's voice was sarcastic.

"When are they going to shut that alarm off?" Missy asked. She was still holding her ears.

"Oh, my head aches," Zoe complained.

"What are you saying, Zoe?" Missy asked.

"I said I have another migraine," Zoe shouted impatiently.

"Oh boy," Susan complained, "look who got called out to be our fire marshal this time. As if you haven't seen enough of him lately, Laurie."

"Oh, come on, Sue. He's okay."

"Well, Arthur wasn't too happy with you yesterday afternoon after the fire, Laurie. You've got to admit that he's been bugging you since you turned him down for a date."

"Well, Arthur is too, uh, self-confident for me."

"You know how men are," Susan replied simply.

"Oh, girls, listen up, okay," Art's nasal voice shouted.

Melissa jumped.

"You'll have to wait until the officer from the bomb squad is finished with his investigation before it will be safe to go back inside the building. I know it's getting cold out here, so I'll tell you when it's all right to go back in."

As Arthur finished speaking, a groan went out from the three hundred-plus girls that were standing outside Falcon Hall wearing night robes and slippers.

"I wonder if anyone was in the shower when the alarm sounded," Susan asked no one in particular.

"Laurie." Melissa's voice sounded urgent.

"What's the matter, Missy?"

"It was Arthur . . . in my dream. Arthur was the fire marshal in my nightmare. It was the same voice."

"Well, that's normal. He is a fire marshal," Laurie said.

"Yeah, I know, but . . ." Melissa sighed. It really wasn't important anyway, she thought. No one wanted to hear about her dream.

"I wish they'd hurry up," Zoe complained. "It's cold out here, and my head is killing me."

Finally, Arthur Wills returned to announce the good news that there was no bomb and they could all go back inside. It was another false alarm.

"Thank you, Lord. Amen," Melissa breathed.

3

Meaningful Meetings

Although the next few days had passed without incident, Zoe was still uneasy.

"Missy, I really don't want to go with you to that Christian meeting tonight," she protested over supper.

"It might help take your mind off things." Then Laurie Gibbs added, "Besides, we will be doing a lot of singing tonight and not a long Bible study."

"Hello, ladies. May I join you?" Alex was smiling his warm, pleasing smile. "I hope this isn't a gathering for a used-book sale with all the Bibles on this table. Missy, you don't mind if I sit next to you?"

"Oh, yes—I mean, no. Uh, that is . . . sit down, Alex. Someday I'll get my foot out of my mouth."

"And you're an English major, Melissa," Zoe scolded.

Alex was still looking at Melissa. "That's all right. We all have our little hang-ups."

Missy wondered what this kind, sensitive, intelligent, athletic, and strong man could possibly have for a hang-up.

"You just got here in time for supper," Laurie commented.

Alex nodded while sawing his way through his ham and then proceeded to eat some baked potato and green beans.

"Alex, you still have half an hour to eat before the meeting," Missy reminded him. She sipped her tea and then nibbled at her roll.

"Mmm. I know," he answered after gulping his tea. "Missy, could you help me tonight setting up and taking down the folding chairs for the meeting, if you don't mind."

"Sure, I'd be glad to." Her eagerness was evident.

"Alex," Laurie said, "maybe you can convince Zoe to come to the fellowship meeting with us tonight."

Zoe raised her hand to protest.

"If she's smart and would like some company of good friends to take her mind off tensions, she'll come." Alex gave Zoe a tender smile. "No need to twist her arm. But then, on the other hand, if she wants to be alone with her problems, she won't come."

"Well, since you put it that way, Alex, how can I refuse?"

During the opening singing, the easy companionship of the group puzzled Zoe. How could these people seem so happy while in the midst of unexpected bomb threats? Not to mention her own haunting dream and the unsettling nightmare that Missy had experienced. The bookstore basement fire was as yet unsolved, she remembered. Added to this was the possibility of the escaped mental patient who might find his way back to Iandale. Zoe breathed a quiet sigh as her eyes read the song lyrics without her mind consciously registering them. Yet there was an unmistakable difference about this little gathering of about twenty odd students. Even the look of joy and contentment that radiated from Melissa's face was disturbing.

After the singing, Alex opened with prayer. Then he

announced, "Before we begin our study in First John tonight, there is a friend of a friend here whom I want to introduce to all of you."

Oh, no. Here it comes. He is going to put me on the spot, Zoe thought to herself. *I knew I shouldn't have come here. I don't need anybody anyway. Missy means well, but...*

"Tonight," Alex continued, "we have an opportunity to obey Jesus's primary commandment. If you like, call it the Eleventh Commandment: to love your neighbor as yourself. We all know the girls on campus in particular have been under some terrible stresses lately with most of the obscene phone calls and bomb threats occurring in the girls' dorms. After the meeting, I'd like you to make a special effort to welcome Zoe Babette. Zoe, I'm not trying to embarrass you. I just want you to know that we care about you in friendship."

"Now let's turn to the first letter of John chapter 4, and please stand as we read this love chapter together," Alex Marcus concluded.

Arthur Wills handed Zoe a Bible, which he had opened to the proper place. He gave her a friendly pat on the shoulder, along with a friendly smile.

Zoe put one hand to her throat as she read. Except for the vibrations that she felt, she could not distinguish her own voice from the oneness of the whole group. She was beginning to feel as though she truly belonged here. The words beckoned her to reach out beyond herself.

Alex continued to speak after a pause when the reading had finished.

"This goes without saying, but I'll say it anyway. You know that 'love your brother' means to care for all people, not just those in your family or those you know and like. It also means to care and pray for your enemies too. We sometimes forget that, don't we? Remember that Jesus treated all people with loving-kindness, even the Roman soldiers. Well, I promised that we'd do more singing this meeting, so let's have some requests now."

Missy's heart skipped a beat as Alex reached for his guitar. His soft voice was clear and low pitched enough that she could hear it well with concentration and a little added volume to her hearing aids.

Peter Early suggested singing "What a Friend We Have in Jesus" to welcome a new friend.

Next Arthur Wills requested "Onward Christian Soldiers."

Zoe found each song easily since the appropriate number was cited along with the title. She was beginning to like this new feeling of belonging.

However, during the singing of "Amazing Grace," which was picked by Laurie Gibbs, Zoe became aware of a knot tightening in her stomach. By the time Alex had sung "Because He Lives" in a beautiful but disquieting solo and Missy had asked for "Just As I Am," Zoe found herself anxiously looking toward the door of the recreation room where the meeting was being held. She wished the meeting would end. Zoe half-expected the walls to begin closing in around her. The sense of belonging had given way to a growing fear of being singled out, like an outsider who was trying to fit in.

Finally, Alex suggested closing with "He Lives."

Zoe rubbed a sweaty palm across her forehead. Finally, she would be able to leave. The desire to escape was overpowering. But escape from what? At the end of Alex's closing prayer, Zoe darted for the door.

Noticing her quick exit, Arthur followed.

"Zoe, wait up. Hey, let me walk you back to the dorm. It's late, and you shouldn't be out at night alone, you know."

"I can take care of myself," Zoe snapped defensively. Then,

after remembering the obscene phone caller, bomb threats, and the recent fire too, she thought better of her hasty remark and added, "Well, all right."

He extended his arm to her. She slipped her hand under it as they began to walk toward the outside.

"I just wanted to get out of there," Zoe confessed.

"I noticed," Arthur replied.

"What's that supposed to mean?"

"Hey, don't chew me out, Zoe. I'm not the one you are fighting against."

"Don't use your psychology on me, Arthur Wills."

"You'll make the right choice sooner or later, Zoe. The right decision must prevail no matter what. You'll do what you must do."

Zoe stopped walking and pulled her arm free. His words stung as much as the cold night air.

"Zoe, what on earth is wrong?"

"Art, you just used an exact quote from this recurring nightmare that haunts me. You scared me half to death."

"Okay, Zoe, take it easy. Probably your subconscious is trying to make you remember something, maybe unpleasant. Just take one step at a time, and things will have a way of falling into place. Justice must prevail, however long it takes."

"You mean, the end justifies the means?"

"Something like that. Come on, Zoe, let's get going."

The group had dispersed, and Missy was helping Alex fold chairs.

"Alex, I wonder if I didn't stick my foot in my mouth again. Zoe wasn't too happy when she ran out of here tonight."

"Oh, you saw her too. She'll probably understand your motivation. She knows you have a caring heart."

"Thanks, Alex." Missy smiled. "You're being generous. But

good intentions don't always justify your actions."

"You, dear Missy, need to learn how to take a compliment." He smiled at her for a long moment. Then his expression changed, although she couldn't see it.

"Alex." She paused. He didn't seem to be aware that she was speaking. She tried again, louder, more deliberately.

"What?"

"Are you okay, Alex?"

"Yeah, I'm fine. Let's sit down a minute now that the extra chairs are all put away." He led her toward a couch on the back wall of the recreation room.

"Alex, do you have any idea who started the bookstore fire yet?"

"No, but the police and administration are cooperating in an investigation. We don't even know if it is the same person who is making the bomb threats and phone calls. I can't imagine why anyone would do such terrible, senseless things."

It was Missy's turn to smile. "Sweet Alex. You are always trying to find the good in people. Sometimes you have to see the bad."

"Melissa . . . I could almost . . ." Alex cupped her chin gently with his hands and tilted her face upward. He lowered his face to gaze intently into hers, but she could not see the expression in his eyes. He repeated her name, savoring it like a piece of delicious candy.

"You are such a special lady, and you don't even realize it, Melissa."

Melissa dared not speak, dared not breathe. Her emotions were all screaming at her at once. She felt warmth and dread, elation and bewilderment, longing and restraint—all in a turmoil of confusion.

Abruptly, Alex dropped his hands and leaned back against

the couch cushion.

"It's getting late. I guess I'd better walk you back to Falcon Hall, Missy."

She looked away, hoping that he wouldn't see the disappointment she felt. "I guess so. That is, if you wouldn't mind."

"My pleasure." His warm smile returned.

The next morning, the alarm clock rudely awakened Missy and Zoe.

"No nightmares, Zo?"

"No, thank God, and no bomb threats either."

"Amen."

"Will you stop that, Missy? You know what I mean."

Zoe went to her closet and chose a kelly green dress that accented her eyes. She began to gather her hairbrush, toothbrush, soap, and towel for her morning trip to the girls' bathroom down the hall.

"What's the occasion?" Missy asked, noticing the dress.

"Huh? Oh. I have an appointment with Dr. Francis this morning."

Promptly at 9:00 a.m., Zoe knocked and then entered the office of Dr. Barbara Francis in the Parker House building on campus. Zoe noticed a startled look on the older woman's face as she sat down in front of her desk.

Dr. Francis smiled weakly. "Well, I have your file here, and I would like to ask you a few questions. Now, where are you from, Ms. Babette?"

"Manchester, New Hampshire."

"There was some mix-up with your records as I recall?"

"It was my understanding that the orphanage would supply the needed information since I had needed it for the scholarships that I won in high school as well. Sister Ruth gave me my Social Security card, but I never got a copy of my birth certificate. She said that she would handle all the details and that I really wouldn't need it for enrollment. Why are you asking me all this now?"

"Just routine. Were you born in Manchester, Ms. Babette?"

Zoe nodded.

"Your parents. Do you know who they were?"

"I never knew anything about my parents, just the orphanage."

"I see."

There was a pause. Dr. Francis straightened in her chair. Zoe noticed the relaxation and congeniality now in her voice when she spoke again.

"You have come a long way then, Ms. Babette. How do you like school so far?"

"It's all right. I enjoy my English classes, especially your creative writing class, Dr. Francis. Of course, we could do without the bomb threats and fire scares though."

"Yes, that is terribly unfortunate. Are you having any other problems, Ms. Babette?"

Zoe shook her head to dismiss the question. She didn't like discussing personal problems with acquaintances.

"Well, remember, if you need any help, you can come to me. That's what I am here for. I would like to ask you one more question if you don't mind."

"Sure, what is it?"

"Your necklace is very . . . unique, Ms. Babette. Where did you get it?"

"Sister Ruth gave it to me when I left to come to Iandale. She said it had belonged to my mother and she wanted me to have it."

When she stood, Dr. Francis extended her right hand to Zoe

as she clutched her chest with the other.

"Thank you for coming by." Dr. Francis's voice took on its earlier hesitation. "Come back if you have questions."

"Thank you. I will, Dr. Francis. See you in class."

Zoe half-closed the door as she pulled it behind her when she fled the office. She almost ran down the corridor toward the outside door of the building. She yanked the double doors open and collided with Alexander Marcus.

"Woa, Zoe. Are you okay?" Alex smiled politely as he held onto her shoulders to brace her.

"Oh, gee, I'm sorry, Alex. I was in a hurry."

"I can see that." He chuckled. "What time are you and Missy going to lunch? You two usually eat together, don't you?"

She nodded and grinned. "Probably around twelve thirty."

"May I meet you in the dining area, say on the right side?"

"Sure thing, Alex. We'll see you there."

As Alex strolled through Parker House, he overheard Dr. Francis talking on the telephone when he was passing by her office. He didn't intend to listen, but her words aroused his curiosity.

"Todd, it's about that freshman girl Zoe Babette. Please, darling, can't you cut your business short and come home sooner? . . . Well, I can't talk about it over the phone . . . Todd, she's wearing the beehive necklace too. It must be her. What do you mean? I just finished speaking with her here in my office . . . Well, I am upset! She was just as uncomfortable as I was . . . Todd . . . Just come home as soon as you can, please, darling . . . Yes, yes, goodbye."

Alex continued to walk on through the building. *What's eating Dr. Francis?*

He wondered what was so special about that cute little necklace Zoe always wears. Didn't he have enough to worry about with the bomb threats plaguing the women and now an arson? He thought of the unnecessary tension that Melissa was being subjected to. She had two physical disadvantages, not that it mattered to him. How would she react when he told her? He shook his head as if to clear his thoughts. She was different from the other girls that he had dated. Her caring was open and honest. Her naivety warmed his heart.

Better get to class, he reminded himself.

"What's for lunch, Zo?" Missy asked as they stood in the right-hand line at the dining commons.

"Tossed salad, American chop suey, corn bread, and Jell-O," a soft, clear male voice from behind her answered.

Missy turned to look up into the smiling face of Alex. She smiled in turn and greeted him warmly. "Hi, Alex. How are you today? You were kind of tired last night."

"Nothing like a good night's sleep. And how are you, pretty lady?"

"Fine, thanks. Uh, doesn't Zoe look pretty?"

"I wasn't looking at Zoe, Melissa."

She flushed slightly and looked away from him.

"Hey, hey, you two, move along. You're holding up the line," Zoe reminded them.

Melissa stepped to the serving area and proceeded to push her tray along and take her lunch. At the end of the line, she removed her tray and stood aside, waiting for Alex and Zoe.

"You go ahead, Alex. I'll follow you to a table."

Alex walked ahead of the girls and chose a table next to the window that looked out onto the school gymnasium.

Zoe teased Melissa as they walked slowly toward the table. "So I'd say it's more than just getting in good with the group leader, hey, Missy?"

"Come on, Zo."

"Missy, if you can't see that he's got eyes for you, then you're blinder than I thought."

"And what are you girls cooking up?" Alex asked.

"Oh, just girl talk," Zoe answered him as she sat down. "Where is Art?"

"He said he was going to the Iandale Public Library to do some structural research. He should be around later. That is a cute necklace, Zoe. Do you keep pictures in it?"

"No, and you are the second person today who has asked me about it," Zoe answered defensively. "I've had a rotten morning. Dr. Francis makes me very uneasy. There is something unsettling about her. Alex, I happen to enjoy studying about bees. My locket has a tiny plastic queen bee inside. That's all."

"Just curious, Zoe. It looks nice with that pretty green dress. Missy, I wanted to ask you to study with me for that psych test tomorrow if you'd like to."

"Oh. I can't tonight, Alex. I'm really sorry. I'm doing my case study report for our counseling class on Joe Burns's granddaughter, Ashley. He said I could interview her tonight at their house on Pine Street."

"I didn't know that Mr. Burns has a grandchild."

Missy nodded, and a piece of Jell-O plopped onto her tray. "Oops. Just call me clux."

"That's kay–el–u–tee–zee," Zoe spelled.

"Whatever. I feel like that character in the old maid card game sometimes, Tilly Tumble."

"Never mind, Missy. You have a beautiful name," Alex said.

4

No Answer

Alex paced around his room at Stanton House. He wished that Art would come back. He needed to toss some ideas around. There were too many questions without answers. How long did this madness have to continue before it would be solved? It was difficult enough for the girls, but Melissa had an even greater disadvantage. This was getting him nowhere.

Alex dropped into the chair in front of his desk. He pulled open his psychology book. He stared at it for a few minutes. Then he pushed it closed in favor of his Bible. He opened it to his favorite passage, Proverbs 3:5-6. He recited it without looking at the words. Then he sighed.

Aloud, he prayed, "Lord, Lord, lead me in the direction of your righteousness. Teach me your wise counsel, Lord, and direction, in Jesus's name. Amen."

Finally, the door clicked open, and the tall, slender figure of Art Wills entered.

"Hey, Art, I'm glad to see you."

"What's the matter, Alex? No date tonight?"

"No. Missy went to Joe Burns's house to interview his granddaughter for our case study assignment."

"Oh, she did?" Art interrupted.

"Yeah. Art, I really need to talk to you. Are you free?"

"I guess I can lend you my ear for a little while, but I have to go out again. What's on your mind, buddy?"

"A lot of things. Art, what do you know about Zoe?"

"Not much, really. Why?"

"I overheard Dr. Francis talking to her husband on the telephone, and she was very upset. It had something to do with that cute brown necklace that Zoe always wears."

Art laughed. "Maybe it's a hornet's nest. Why don't you talk to Dr. Francis's husband about it? I just saw him in the coffee shop at the Student Center."

"You did?" Alex sounded surprised. "So he did come back early after all. Art, do you think the bomb threats and the fire were caused by the same person?"

"Why not?"

"I just wish that we had a clue by now. What do you think, Art? You're the psychology major."

"I think you think too much." Arthur grinned. "Here, Alex, have a piece of butterscotch candy."

Alex took it and began to absentmindedly twist the yellow cellophane wrapper between the fingers of his left hand.

"Don't worry, Alex. Things have a way of working out right. Go ahead. Eat your candy. It doesn't have a bug in it."

"Huh? Oh, yeah. Thanks. Tell me, Art, what do you think of Melissa Sanders?"

"Are you sure you want my honest opinion, ol' buddy?"

"Of course."

"I think she should stay with her own kind."

"What do you mean?"

"Handicapped people should be put in group homes where they can be taken care of. They have enough problems without trying to mingle with the rest of us."

"Arthur Wills, I am surprised at you. How can you say that? All people have a right to a better quality life no matter what their circumstances."

"All right. Take an example from the Bible," Art argued. "Look at the blind man outside the Temple in the Gospel accounts. He kept shouting to Jesus even though he was told to be quiet, and finally, Jesus healed him. You know as well as I do the verses that talk about being well or healthy."

"You are confusing illness with disability, Art. Where did you get such a negative opinion of handicapped people anyway?"

"I knew a blind girl in high school named Clarissa Mandez who was like your goody-goody Melissa Sanders. She'll be another old maid. You know, Alex, false humility is as much a sin as boasting. Melissa has a problem with false humility, or haven't you noticed? Take off your blinders and see what you are getting into, buddy."

"I am aware of her disabilities, Art. In spite of them, she is still a woman, a very unique woman. Tell me about this girl Clarissa."

Arthur turned and strode toward the door of their room. He gripped the doorknob and twisted it open. With his back to Alex, he spoke quickly, slurring his words.

"Maybe some other time, Alex. I have to go."

Bang. The door was shut.

Alex was left alone with his thoughts. *Shows how much you know about people.* Alex sighed.

He stood and began to pace the room again. He reassured himself that Melissa would understand. Surely, she wouldn't react as the other girls had before. He stopped in front of his desk and pulled his psychology book from the stack on the left-hand corner. Alex set the book on the desk in front of him and stared into its cover.

Melissa shouldn't be out alone at night, he thought.

He hoped Zoe had gone with her to Joe's house. The chair scraped the floor as Alex pulled it back from the desk to sit down again. He propped one elbow onto the desk and rested his chin in his hand. With his left hand, Alex opened his psychology book to study.

Later Alex plumped his book closed and got up to stretch. He stepped over to his bed to look at his clock radio. The time was after 11:25 p.m. After pausing for a moment, he decided to go to the pay phone in the hall near the bathroom. He dialed the number for Falcon Hall.

"Zoe Babette, please. This is Alexander Marcus."

Moments dragged.

"Don't tell me you are calling to say there is another bomb threat? The alarm is broken, right?"

"Very funny, Zoe. Is Missy there?"

"No, she isn't back yet."

"You didn't go with her?"

"No, Alex, she knows her way to Pine Street."

"Can you give me Joe Burns's phone number?"

Alex thanked her then hung up to dial the number she had given him. One long *burr–ring*. Pause. Another long ring. Pause. A third ring suddenly stopped. Then nothing.

Again Alex punched the buttons on the phone. No *burr–ring*. There was no sound at all. Upon slamming the receiver back onto its cradle, Alex ran through the hall and down the stairs to exit Stanton House.

5

Old Maid

Missy arrived at Joe Burns's house about 7:15 p.m. His light-blue ranch at the end of Pine Street was easy to spot because it stood next to a wooded lot, which had become a favorite playground for neighborhood youngsters. Missy was glad she walked frequently around the college town. She knew the area, and she was confident that she could find her way back to the dorm in the evening darkness. She had walked the half block from her dorm to Center Street and, turning left, had followed it through the main part of town—past the closed stores, the hospital, and past the large brick church that stood as a statement of faith at the head of the town square. Moving along, passing homes, she had stopped at each street, crossing to read the signs when she stood under them.

Thank God for streetlights, she had mused.

Finding Pine Street, she crossed it and turned left to go down to the last house on the right side, number 836. Now she rapped on the white front door.

Upon entering the living room, Missy could see a slim,

blond figure sitting on the floor in front of the fireplace. She made no move although she must have heard the front door open and close. Her gaze seemed to be transfixed on the burning logs. Missy could not see the captivated look in the young girl's blue-gray eyes as she sat fascinated by the crackling flames.

"Come into the kitchen, Ms. Sanders. I need to talk with you."

Recalling her thoughts, Missy replied, "Please call me Missy. My friends do."

"All right, and I guess you can call me Joe on one condition." He stood behind the kitchen chair, waiting.

"What's that?"

"Do you play cards? I mean, can you see well enough?"

Sitting opposite his chair, she nodded. Then she reached into her purse and promptly produced a small box for him to see.

"I have my own deck with larger printed numbers, which is easier for me to see, but I can use the regular decks also." She smiled and then said, "My favorite game is cribbage. What's yours, Joe?"

This question produced a smile from his lined face. "Old maid," he responded and pulled out his chair to sit down.

"You see," Joe paused, sighed, and then drew in a deep breath to continue, "after my son and his wife died in the car wreck a few years ago, Ashley was almost six, I used to play old maid with her, you know, to help take her mind off," he hesitated momentarily, "things. Got so I'm kinda partial to the game now."

The chair moaned when Joe shifted his weight.

Missy nodded. She placed the deck of cards in the middle of the table and withdrew her hand to fold them in her lap.

Joe affixed his eyes to the box and continued to explain.

"Ashley and I have to take care of each other now. It took a long time for both of us to get used to being alone—especially since my wife died a short time after the accident. Doctors say she had a heart attack."

Missy could hear the inflection in his voice as he hurried to finish.

"She never was sick much. It happened sudden. I think she died of a broken heart. You want some tea, Missy?"

Joe abruptly pushed back his chair and turned his attention to filling the teapot.

Missy allowed several minutes for Joe to collect himself then asked, "Joe, what caused the accident?"

"Drunk driver!" He hurled the words at the wall. Even though his back was turned, Missy heard it clearly. Finally, when he came back to the table with their tea, he added, "A drunken driver hit Jimmy's car head-on. He showed up on Jimmy's side of the road comin' round a turn. Police said they never knew what hit 'em. It was that fast. The other guy was killed too. I'm glad of that. I can't see why God had to take them all away from me—from Ashley and me." The older man pulled a handkerchief from his plaid shirt pocket to wipe his eyes. Then he sipped his tea, black.

Missy concentrated on dunking her tea bag. "Joe, was Ashley in the car at the time?"

"No!" The word was a sharp, angry protest. After a few moments, Joe cleared his throat and lowered his voice. "No. Ashley was staying with Martha and me. Her folks—my son, Jimmy, and his wife, Helen—were goin' off together for a weekend trip. We never expected them to . . . to go away for good."

Missy set her cup down to respond. "Unfortunately, we don't always understand God's purpose." She sighed and then asked, "Joe, have you ever read about heaven in the Bible?"

"Of course I have," he retorted angrily. After a moment, he spoke more normally. "Ya, I was a Christian. My whole family is. I trusted Jesus Christ. That is, until the accident. Never could understand why he allowed it to happen. A tragic waste, was all."

"Joe, you are only seeing one side—the hurt side. If you know about heaven and what a beautiful and peaceful place it must be, imagine your family there. Don't forget, you will be reunited with Martha, Jimmy, and Helen when it is in God's timing. Joe, the accident was just the beginning for them—not the end."

"Hmp. That's quite a mouthful, young lady. That may be easy for you to say, but it doesn't change things now."

"Yes, I know, but Jesus didn't promise that the road would always be easy. He experienced the death of a friend and heartache too. Remember, Jesus gave up his own life so that we might gain life eternal through his death and resurrection. Joe, don't lose sight of the blessed hope of eternal life with your family in heaven. Look to Jesus to heal your hurt so that you can see heaven more clearly."

"Look who is talkin' about seein' more clearly."

Missy smiled at his obvious dig.

"There is one more thing I have to tell you before you talk to Ashley. Ever since the accident, she has been fascinated by fire. Doctors say it is a psychological thing because the vehicles burst into flames immediately when they hit." His voice faltered. Finally, he added, "She'll just sit there in front of the fireplace for hours and just watch the flames. I guess it is her way of workin' it out with herself." He sighed again. "You had to know."

"Would you rather I don't ask her about this?"

Joe shrugged his shoulders. "Doesn't matter, I guess. You'd

better go and talk to her now. I'll be putting her to bed soon. Then we'll have a couple of games of cards, if you don't mind playin'." He rested his chin in his hand, which was propped up by his elbow on the table.

"Sure, Joe." She gave him a smile before turning to leave the room, but he didn't return it. His eyes were downcast.

Missy came into the living room from across the hall and sat down beside Ashley on the blue-and-gold swirl carpet in front of the hearth. After a few moments, Missy made an attempt to speak to the young girl.

"How are you, Ashley? I'm Melissa Sanders, but my friends call me Missy."

No response.

"Ashley?" Missy reached out and touched the slim arm.

"Huh?" Her face turned toward the unheeded presence. "Oh, you must be the lady Grandpa told me about."

"Yes, I'm Melissa Sanders, but my friends call me Missy."

"You're kinda pretty, but what happened to your eye?"

"It has been like this since I was born." Missy began to explain as simply as she could to this nine-year-old. "You see, I was born too early, premature. For the first couple of months, the doctors gave me oxygen to keep me alive, but they didn't realize to cover my eyes for protection since they were not fully developed. Around ten years later, they discovered that too much oxygen damages the optic and auditory nerves."

"That's for your eyes and your ears," Ashley interrupted.

Missy smiled patiently and then answered, "That's right. I have a little sight in my right eye, and I wear hearing aids in both ears to make sounds louder and easier to hear. I have never seen anything with my left eye, not even light from the sun or darkness at night. Also, like you, I am the only child in my family. So I guess we have something in common."

"And you had an accident when you were born. My mommy and daddy had an accident too. Did my grandpa tell you?"

Missy nodded.

Ashley explained, "My mommy and daddy had a car accident, and they went to be with Jesus."

"Yes, I know." Missy blinked and squeezed her eyes shut to fight back the threatening tears. "Do you know Jesus too?"

The younger girl nodded slowly and deliberately in deep bowing fashion for Missy to see it. She had only taken her eyes off the fire momentarily when she first looked at the intruder. Her gaze had not left the flames since.

"Ashley, do you mind that your parents and Grandma went to heaven?"

Her petite shoulders lifted slightly, and Missy saw the movement.

"Well, I miss them a lot, but I guess it's okay 'cause heaven is such a nice place to be. I can't wait until I can see them again, but I like it here too. I don't want to go to heaven yet."

"I understand, Ashley."

"How come you are doing a report on me for school?"

"Well, I have to do a case study, a history of a real chi—uh, young person's life, and since I don't know too many people around Iandale, your grandpa said I could ask you."

"Oh. Where are you from?"

"I was born and grew up in Manchester, New Hampshire. Have you ever been there, Ashley?"

Ashley nodded. "Ya, when I was around five, I think, we all went there for a circus, and sometimes Grandpa takes me shopping there. We go for the whole day and eat out. I like that. Don't you?"

Missy nodded, smiling. "Now, where were you born

Ashley?"

"I was born in Newark, New Jersey, but I was still a baby when we moved here though. Grandpa quit being a taxi driver, and Daddy got an offer from the company that makes boots in Iandale, so we moved all at the same time to here."

"Your dad was a factory worker? Didn't he have a better job in Newark?"

Her ashen-blond hair flew wildly as Ashley shook her head vigorously. "No. Daddy was the boss. He went to college like you did. Mommy went to college too, but she didn't work. She took care of me."

"Oh. Were you a handful?" Missy teased.

"I don't know." Ashley shrugged her shoulders and turned back to the fire.

Missy prayed silently while she and Ashley sat in front of the fire's glowing heat. She prayed that God, in His goodness, would heal Joe's wounded heart and open his eyes to Jesus's loving, healing tenderness. She prayed for God's loving hand on Ashley's life and that His strength of faith would grow strong in her. Then she prayed for God to lead Alex and Art in their attempts to help solve the mystery of the phone calls and the bomb scares. Finally, Missy sighed as if to cast all her cares upon Him.

"Ashley, what is so fascinating about the fire?"

"I don't know. I like to watch it. It reminds me of people dancing and dreaming."

"Hmm. It's like a secret place to be alone with your thoughts, huh?" Missy interpreted.

"Ya, that's it." Ashley was evidently pleased that someone else understood her. She turned to glance briefly at the older female. "I like you, Missy. Would you be my friend?"

"Yes. I'd love to be your friend. Ashley, if you ever need

someone to talk to, I'm a very quiet listener, okay?"

"Ya. Are your mommy and daddy still alive?"

"Yes, and one set of grandparents too. I never knew my father's parents because they died before I was born."

"Me too," Ashley responded quickly, but her gaze never left the flames. "Grandpa and me are pals now. Right, Grandpa?"

She stood and went to the older man who had just entered the room. He greeted her with a hug and a smile.

"It's gettin' near bedtime, Sunshine," he reminded her.

"May I have a hug too?" Missy asked.

Ashley turned her questioning blue-gray eyes up into the man's lined face. "Grandpa, is Missy your friend too?"

He nodded.

"Then I guess it's okay." She walked over to Missy, who gave her a tight squeeze and a kiss on the cheek.

"Good night, Ashley, and thank you for the interview."

"It was kinda fun. Night, Grandpa. Night, Missy."

After Ashley had gone down the hall, Joe turned to Missy and suggested, "Now, how about that game of old maid you promised?"

Missy smiled and followed Joe into the kitchen. She could see that he had been preparing. On the table he had set their cups of tea, a deck of cards, and in the center, a plate of store-bought cookies. Missy had always felt more comfortable with people older than herself. She had guessed it to be a sense of security. She fell into a relaxed state as they played one game after another. Time passed without notice.

"Hmp," Joe mused. "I've got a pair here of Barb Dwire. You know, barbed wire. Reminds me of my boss Mr. McGuire. He keeps buggin' me about retirin'."

"You are snappy sometimes yourself, Joe," Missy reminded. After a moment, she added, "Don't let him be a thorn in your side. Just tell him that you are doing your best. That's what counts. People complain about me being slow too, and I'm only nineteen."

"You know, I see some of Helen in you, young lady." Joe smiled a little. "She was an encourager."

"Helen?" Missy looked up from her cards. "Oh, you mean your daughter-in-law. Thank you, Joe. Ah, I have a pair of Art Smarts." She sighed as she laid the cards down. "I pray that Art and Alex will come up with some evidence soon to help solve the mystery at school."

"Come to think of it, I seem to see you and Alex together a lot on campus. Anything serious between you two?"

Missy's laugh was a sound of pleasure. "You sound like my roommate Zoe. The truth is, I like Alex a lot, but we are just close friends."

"Sure. That's what they all say at first," he retorted.

"No, really. I do like Alex a lot, but I can't think of getting serious now. Right now I have a career to think about. I want to earn my bachelor's degree in teaching before I do anything else. You know, one thing at a time. I have enough to take care of myself, never mind anybody else. I'm not ready for a commitment yet, and I haven't even talked about it with him."

"Women. Think you have all the answers, don't you?"

She giggled. "Oh, no. I've already been pegged Tilly Tumble. Why, even Art calls me a goody-goody old maid." Her expression sobered behind the cards, which she held up in front of her nose. "I probably won't ever get married anyway."

Burr-ring.

Joe got up from his chair when the telephone rang a second time. He wondered who would call him at this hour. The third ring was cut short by abrupt darkness.

A scream from the direction of the living room was

followed by several loud bangs. Then a deafening crashing sound and the unmistakable crackling of fire confronted them.

"Grandpa! Grandpa!" Ashley shrieked.

Upon opening the living room door, Joe and Missy stared into a living nightmare. A flaming tree had crashed through the roof of the house. Its branches stretched into the rear of the room, beckoning with its fiery fingers amid shingles, plaster and wood and debris. At the opposite end of the room, fire had started where a log from the still-burning fireplace lay on the rug. Ashley was shivering in the corner with the fireplace, poker clutched in her hands. She was sobbing uncontrollably and mumbling that she didn't mean to.

"Ashley! Break the window and go outside!" Joe yelled.

She did not move.

Quickly, Missy crossed the room and grasped hold of the younger girl's arm. "Ashley, come with me."

Missy pried the poker loose from frigid fingers and then tugged at her arm to get Ashley to move. The black smoke, which was being hurled toward the front of the house by the wind, made it difficult to see. Missy's eyes burned, and the stench of petroleum added to the nauseous feeling. While holding Ashley close to her body, Missy crossed the room between the burning log and the tall flames from the other end.

Seconds seemed to be hours until the three of them were safely outside huddled together at the edge of the sidewalk.

Joe could hear an approaching siren from the distance. "God, please help me." He sobbed.

6

Smoke Rises

Alex was glad he had brought his 18 speed Schwinn Paramount bicycle to school with him for exercise as well as for pleasure riding. It would certainly save him time now. When he turned onto Center Street, he realized that he didn't know which house on Pine Street belonged to Joe Burns. From the main street, he could turn either right or left onto it, since it was a cross street father up past the business section of town. While riding he remembered the park that ran adjacent to Center Street about a block above it to the right. He knew he had seen a telephone booth there, which, he hoped, held a directory. When he neared the central part of town, Alex turned right onto Iandale Drive, which proceeded downhill on one side of the public common and extended out into another rural residential area in town. He then turned left onto Park Street, which stretched the length of the common and beyond. He slowed to park his bicycle as he approached the midsection of the common.

Alex was surprised and dismayed to notice that the phone

booth was occupied when he arrived. He busied himself locking his bike to the leg of a park bench at the edge of the grass. Momentarily, however, the door of the phone booth pushed open, and a tall figure wrestled his way out of the enclosure. Under the streetlight Alex caught a glimpse of the tall man hurrying away in the same direction from which he had just come. A plaid hunter's cap hid the man's hair, but a thicket of brown about the cheek indicated a bushy beard. His tattered jeans and dusty boots contrasted with the London Fog raincoat. The man resembled Todd Francis, Alex thought, but what would he be doing out here at a pay phone at this hour of the night? Alex dismissed the thought and entered the booth more easily than the stranger had exited it. He opened the directory to the B section of the white pages and dug in his pants pocket for his pen light. As he read through the list of names, he was surprised to see the name of "Babette, Dennis" listed once. To his chagrin, there were several Joseph Burns listed, but only one on Pine Street, at number 836.

Quickly Alex closed the book, pushed open the door, and went to unlock his bike. While mounting he heard the unmistakable wail of a siren. He was still on Iandale Drive when he saw the fire engine heading down Center Street in the direction from which he had come. Indecision struck him. Should he go back to the campus? Instead, he turned right almost automatically when he came to Center Street. Another fire truck screamed past him, but this one was traveling in the same direction as Alex. His heart began to race. The next were the fire engine and the police car; surely they weren't all going to Pine Street?

As Alex turned left onto Pine Street, he could now see the black smoke and flashing lights coming from the far end. A police cruiser sped away from the scene as he approached. It

The Purging Fire

was carrying Joe, Ashley, and Missy to the Iandale Hospital.

Alex parked his bike and approached the fireman who was holding a portable radio in one hand and the truck mike in the other. Alex offered his assistance. "May I help? I'm a fire marshal for the college."

"You're a little late. Damage is already done."

"Was anyone injured? I'm looking for a friend of mine who was visiting here." Alex followed the man's example and turned his back to the wind. His stomach muscles began to tighten.

"Just missed 'em. The police escorted the three occupants to the hospital to check 'em over. Lucky they got out in time. We had a hot one going here."

"Do you think it was set deliberately?"

"Don't know yet, but you can bet that tree had some help other than the wind bein' in the right direction at the time. Hey, Paul, take this college kid over with you to investigate the debris for evidence." He looked Alex straight in the eyes and held up a finger. "Now, you don't touch a thing. Understand?"

He thinks the fire was deliberately set and aided to burn by some accompanying material. Alex's mind began to calculate. Who had that kind of a grudge against Joe Burns? Were they dealing with a compulsive fire setter? If so, could he or she be setting the bomb scares off on campus as well?

Alex could see the charred red paper that Paul was holding up in his gloved hand.

"Simple firecrackers, lots of paper, an old, dry pine tree, and some gasoline to keep the fire speeding." Paul shook his head. "It'll take quite awhile to clean up this mess and rebuild. Shame."

"I know."

Paul added, "I'll check with the police to see if they are checking the woods over there for suspects."

Alex nodded. "Who called you?"

"A police cruiser heading back to the station saw the smoke from Center Street. Good thing he reacted quickly. Let's go. I'm through here for now."

"Yeah," Alex agreed, "this place smells even with the fire out."

"... Wonder none of them were seriously hurt."

The fire chief was wrapping up the preliminary report with the police officer who had returned when Alex and the other fireman rejoined him.

"That college girl got the other folks outside in a hurry, the way I see it. She had more black soot on her from shielding the little girl," the police officer observed.

"Good thing they weren't all asleep," the fire chief added. "Wouldn't have had a chance the way that fire was spreading. The kitchen and bathroom got mainly smoke damage, but the rest..." He gestured a hand out toward the debris.

"Ashley, the little girl, was awake at this time of night?"

The two officials turned to look at Alex who had been standing nearby.

"Seems she had a fire of her own goin'," the fire chief explained. "According to the lady that you must have been lookin' for, she had knocked a log from the fireplace, and it caught on the rug about the same time the other ruckus occurred."

"By the way," Alex added, "I noticed that the electrical and telephone cables on the outside of the house are cut, also deliberately."

The other men were silent, and Alex continued.

"That explains why the phone went dead when I tried to call."

The chief grunted.

"Say, I saw an engine go past me in the opposite direction on my way here. Was it heading for . . ."

Alex didn't have to finish. The firemen were nodding.

"Another false alarm," Paul summed it up.

Alex nodded and thanked them for their prompt timing. Then he left to head up the street for the hospital.

Upon inquiry at the emergency room information station, Alex learned that Joe and Ashley were being kept overnight for observation as a precautionary measure due to age. Missy had been released, at her insistence, only moments before. Looking around, he did not see her. The receptionist assured him that she would have to pass the admittance area to leave and that he could wait. Then he spotted her coming out of the ladies' room.

"Missy, are you all right?"

At the sound of his familiar voice, Missy looked up into concerned blue eyes. Her voice caught on his name, and she couldn't stop the flood of tears that released a torrent of emotions too long held back.

His arms enfolded her. The sound of his voice murmuring incoherently and the steady rise and fall of his chest against her cheek all whispered encouragement and strength.

Her hair felt strawlike as his fingers caressed it. Ignoring the smoky smell, he placed a kiss on her forehead. Missy lifted her face to look up, and his mouth closed over hers in one brief heart-stopping moment. Alex's smile sent her spirits soaring, but when she at last tried to speak, her voice was a faltering whisper.

"Alex, there was a fire . . ."

"I know all about it, honey. Sorry, I didn't get there sooner." He released his hold to put one arm around her waist. "I guess I can at least escort my steady girl home."

Her smile betrayed her pleasure more than her nodding.

When they approached the reception area, Alex noticed his friend standing in front of the receptionist.

"Well, if it isn't Early Bird Pete. What dragged you out at this time of night?"

"I might ask you the same, old buddy. Truth is, my scanner radio just wouldn't keep quiet tonight. Since I was up anyway with the bomb threat at Falcon Hall again, I took a drive past Joe's place—what's left of it—and found that everybody had left already. The next logical place to go was here. How are you doing, Missy?"

"I'm holding up, thanks."

"I see." Pete gave Alex a knowing grin. "I know that Joe and Ashley have already been sedated for the night, so I'll have to get my exclusive interview from you, Missy. How about you two joining me for some pie and coffee at the diner? I bet Missy could use a diversion about now. I've got my car outside."

"Senior privileges," Alex teased.

"But I'm a mess. I don't think so."

"Don't worry about it, Missy. You're fine. Besides, I bet you haven't even been there yet. It's too far to walk out by the highway. Oh, I almost forgot about my bike. Pete, do you think it'll fit in the back of your car?"

"There's only one way to find out. How about it, Missy? My treat for an interview. Okay?"

She sighed. "I guess so."

Soon they were in Pete's car with Alex's bike in the rear compartment heading past the campus Student Union on their way out of town to the only twenty-four-hour restaurant near the interstate highway. It was a sure diversion for state police and other night workers and a reliable source of information for a newspaperman Pete knew.

The diner was quiet and sparsely populated when they

entered.

"Pete, did Art handle the bomb threat?" Alex waited for Missy to slide into the window seat of the booth, and then he sat down beside her.

Pete, who sat opposite them, nodded. "Who else? You weren't around."

"Yeah, I know. The fire truck was heading that way when I was on my way to Joe's."

"Alex, how did you know to come?"

"I tried to call you at the dorm, and Zoe said that you weren't back yet. When I tried to call Joe, the phone was cut off."

"Oh, yes, it did ring, and then . . ." She let her voice trail off.

A waitress that Pete knew brought their menus.

"God certainly watches over us, doesn't He?" Missy asked no one in particular after the waitress had gone. She opened her smoky, smelling purse to get her magnifying glass.

Alex asked, "What would you like to have to eat, honey?"

"I'd like to have this whole mess solved, but I guess I'll settle for some pudding and milk." She looked from Alex to Pete. "Why aren't there any clues?"

"Perhaps we are overlooking them," Pete offered.

Alex sighed. "God knows I've prayed for some answers."

"I'm sorry, Alex." Missy touched his hand, and he held on to hers. "I know it's frustrating for you and Art too. What are you having, Pete?"

"Boston cream pie and coffee," he replied promptly.

Alex teased, "He was just waiting for you to ask." He gave her hand a squeeze. "No tea, Missy?"

She shook her head and leaned close to his ear to whisper that she still felt a little nauseous.

He nodded.

The waitress came to take their orders. Alex ordered the

same items for Missy and himself, and the waitress smiled when Pete added his favorite dessert. Then her expression changed.

"By the way, I heard you people had some excitement on campus earlier tonight."

"Yeah, another bomb scare," Missy returned.

"I mean, besides that," the woman persisted.

"What else did you hear?" Pete asked.

"I overheard two policemen talking about some girl reporting that something was stolen from her room after the alarm."

Even Early Bird Pete raised his eye brows in surprise. Then he asked, "Do you know what it was?"

The waitress shook her head. "Be back with your orders."

Missy pulled her hand free and crossed her arms, hugging her stomach. "Any more bad news?"

"The Burns' house fire was deliberately set." The words were out before Alex thought about it. He tried to add some good news. "Well, some evidence was found in the debris. Some clues are bound to turn up."

With encouragement, Missy retold the nightmare.

Afterward, Alex tried to change the subject by asking, "Missy, does Zoe have any relatives in Iandale?"

"No. I'm sure she doesn't, Alex. Why?"

"Just wondering. I saw the name Babette in the phone book when I was on Park Street looking for Joe's house number."

The waitress brought their snacks.

The milk painted Missy's throat with soothing coolness as it slid downward. She sat quietly, poking at her pudding while Alex and Pete made plans to further investigate the strange events.

"Missy, are you okay?"

"Yeah." She brought her mind back to the present at Alex's

question. "I was just thinking about Ashley. She was really scared. I think she was more upset about accidentally knocking the burning log out of the fireplace though. I guess she couldn't sleep and was watching the fire again."

"Well, she'll be all right now. That's the main thing."

Missy frowned. "Pete, have you heard any news about the escaped mental patient? Has he been apprehended yet?"

"No, I haven't, Missy. I have almost forgotten about that news bulletin. I'll check on it for you." He took the last bite of his pie. "I'm going to have more coffee if you two want anything else?"

Missy got another glass of milk, and Alex ordered tea this time.

"It's time to think more pleasant thoughts, Missy." Alex tried again to be encouraging. "Be transformed by the renewing of your mind so that you may prove what the will of God is, that which is good and acceptable and perfect," Alex quoted.

"Of course." Missy's features relaxed into a smile, and her expression recaptured its enthusiasm. "Romans 12:2. Thank you, sweetheart." The word slipped off her tongue. Her face felt hot.

Alex gave her his reassuring smile and got up to take her hand as she slid out of the booth. The three of them headed out to Pete's red station wagon to ride back to school. Pete parked in front of Falcon Hall and waited while Alex walked Missy inside the lobby.

"Missy, I want you to call me anytime if you need to."

"Yes, I will. I promise. I've already memorized your dorm floor phone number. Don't worry."

He shook his head. "No. You don't worry." Alex bent his head to kiss her. Afterward, she looked around to find no one else in the lobby. "Now you have something else to think about."

He smiled pleasingly.

Missy reached up to put her arms around his neck.

Encouraged by her touch, he tightened his embrace.

"Alex, thank you. I'll never forget tonight."

"Me too," he mumbled. He hugged her again and then gently released his arms. "Better get some sleep. I'll come and get you for breakfast, okay?"

She drew in her breath. "Breakfast. I usually go at seven, and it must be well past midnight. She smiled. "Good night, Alex." After lingering a moment, she went upstairs.

When Missy arrived at her corner room, she was surprised to see a light on and Zoe still up pacing the floor.

"Missy, where have you been? My favorite beehive necklace is gone!"

"What?"

"I took it off to go take a shower. Before I left the room, I put it back in the box in my top bureau drawer. I had barely gotten back here when that stupid fire alarm sounded. When I came back here after the false alarm, it was gone! I was going to report it to Art, but he had already left. I told the policeman. Missy, I have looked everywhere. It is gone!"

"Zoe, I'm going to call Alex. I'll be right back."

7

As the Smoke Thickens

Alex walked Zoe to the Iandale Police Station on Center Street the following morning to formally complete her report of the missing necklace. While there, Alex had an opportunity to study records of both Joe's house fire and the description of the mental patient who was also still missing. On his way back to school, he had stopped at the hospital to inquire about Joe and Ashley. Now he was knocking on the door of his friend Pete Early who lived on the top floor of Stanton House.

"What's the news?" Pete greeted him amiably.

"I'm supposed to ask you that," Alex said and then chuckled. He stretched out in a chair next to Pete's desk.

Pete sat down again and leaned an elbow on a nearby book. "What's so special about that necklace to get Zoe so upset about it anyway? She's always got it on."

"You really have to understand Zoe to know. It's a one-of-a-kind piece from what she tells me a family keepsake."

"Maybe she just misplaced it," Pete suggested. "If it's only valuable to Zoe, it isn't worth stealing in itself."

Alex shrugged his shoulders. "Both girls say they have searched the room more than thoroughly. I don't know."

Pete grinned slyly. "Speaking of Melissa, what's the scoop with you two? I see you've been rather preoccupied lately."

"Preoccupied? Maybe. You know, Pete, I had forgotten about the escaped guy too, until Missy mentioned it last night. I was studying his file at the station this morning. Pete, have you noticed how much his description resembles Todd Francis?"

Pete nodded. "Odd there hasn't been a recent update on his whereabouts. He could be anywhere in the country or out of it by now."

"Pete, he could even be here in Iandale. Last night, on the common, I saw a man coming out of the phone booth who resembled Todd Francis. What if . . ."

"Yup. I follow," Pete cut in. You know, the caller of the bomb threats never stays on the phone long enough for a trace. He probably uses different locations to call from too. I know I would." Then he added, "That is, if I were a criminal. I bet the police were figuring on an inside call, you know, from a building. An outside phone seemed to be too obvious, but I guess not."

"You said we were overlooking the obvious, Early Bird."

"Yup. I guess I did. Hey, let's you and me stake out that phone booth you were talking about on Park Street. Maybe we can spot him making a call."

Alex sat up in his chair. "Good idea. We can take turns each night, and I'll get Art to help too."

"Only thing is, we don't know if he uses the same phone very often, but it's worth a shot."

"I would be so glad to catch that lunatic who is threatening the girls. You notice it is always the girls' dorms that get these threatening calls. I wish I could get Missy out of this situation. I pray every night for God to protect her."

"Take it easy, Alex. Hey, this really is serious between you two, isn't it? Or hasn't she accepted yet?"

"Yeah, Pete. I care for her, but it isn't that simple."

"Why not?"

Alex shifted his weight in the chair and dropped his eyes to study the linoleum pattern. "It's personal. All right. You don't know me as well as you think either."

"I see." There was a pause. Then Pete ventured, "You must be weighing the facts, her handicap and all. Not that I'm holding that against her. She does very well with her limitations, but it sticks in your throat when you say it. You don't have any idea of what it's like to be handicapped.

"Well, Melissa does, and she seems to be handling it. I just meant that you need to walk into this situation with both eyes open, Alex, because she can't."

Alex raised his eyes to meet Pete's gaze. "Yes, I know what you mean, Pete. But it isn't her handicap that bothers me."

"What then?"

Alex sighed and covered his face with his hands for a moment. Then he dropped them in his lap and replied, "This whole mess about bombs and fire alarms bothers me. Missy said she couldn't understand why we didn't have any clues. Maybe I was so obsessed with getting her attention that I overlooked the obvious."

"Overlooked what? The lunatic?"

Alex nodded. "I know it's a long shot. But if the guy I saw wasn't him, it could put Todd Francis in the running. Don't you think so?"

Pete shrugged his shoulders.

"I'd like to talk to the man anyway."

"Now, Alex, don't you go accusing people . . ."

Alex got up and waved a hand in front of Pete's face.

"Stop worrying, Pete. You don't even know what I am talking about. It's just something I overheard awhile back."

"Alex, I was just trying to help." Another few moments of silence passed. Then Pete changed the subject. "So who is going to take the first watch on our stakeout?"

"Sorry I jumped on you, Pete. I've got too many things on my mind these days, I guess. I'll go take the first watch, if you don't mind, and I'll tell Art about it. The guy hasn't called more than a couple of times a week so far. Let's start on Sunday night."

Pete agreed, and Alex left to go find his roommate.

Remembering that Art would be in class in the science building, Alex crossed the street by the Student Union and took a shortcut through Parker House. While approaching Dr. Francis's office to check her office hours, he heard voices coming from inside.

". . . Had better pull yourself together, Barbara," her husband was saying. "You're not doing yourself any good by carrying on this way."

"You still don't see it, do you? Someone else must know. Why else would anyone steal it? The girl told me herself in class this morning that the necklace is missing."

"Stop it, Beebee!"

Alex, who had stopped just short of the office door, heard the stinging blow when the woman's hand struck her husband's face above his bearded cheek.

Then Alex heard her say, "I told you never to call me that again."

The man was mumbling something when Alex walked on.

More questions, he thought to himself. *What's so important about that particular necklace?* He shook his head. Had the necklace originally belonged to Dr. Francis, been lost or stolen, and somehow wound up around Zoe's neck? He hoped Art would have some ideas.

Alex waited outside in the hall when he came to Art's science classroom. His thoughts were jumbled. Would Missy really understand when he told her? Would it be any different this time than in the past? He knew he had never felt this close to a woman before, except his mother, and she was gone now. Missy had to understand. She took her own disabilities in stride, and he thought he did also. Would it really work out for him this time?

Think about something else, he told himself.

He folded his arms across his chest and leaned back against the wall. Now, who would be cruel enough to set a house fire, or senseless enough? Why hadn't there been answers yet? Did he really have a lead on the bomb threats, or was he grasping for nothing?

Alex was so intent on his own thoughts that he didn't even notice his tall, dark roommate until Art tapped him on the shoulder.

"Hey, Alex. What's up?"

"Art, I really need to talk to you. Do you have some free time?"

"Why, Alex, time isn't free."

No reaction.

"Alex, what's the matter with you? That was a joke."

"Huh? Oh, yeah, Art. Do you have some time now?"

"Just so happens you're in luck. I don't have any more classes today. I hope you don't either, by the look on your face. Let's walk back to the room for a while. You look paler than my bedsheets. What's your problem?"

"Let's go this way." Alex pointed toward Parker House when they stepped out into the crisp autumn coldness. "I overheard the Francis's arguing in her office on my way here. I want to talk to Todd if I can catch up with him. They were arguing about Zoe's necklace of all things."

"Zoe's necklace?" Art repeated.

"Yeah, that cute beehive necklace she always wears. Zoe found it missing after the alarm last night. Why that should upset Dr. Francis, I haven't the slightest idea."

Other students and professors were traveling through the faculty office building, and some professors were in their offices, but Dr. Francis and her husband had already left.

Alex and Art crossed the street and turned right.

"That can't be what's eating you, Alex. What else?" Art asked.

"I just came from talking with Pete. We came up with a plan to catch the obscene caller. I think I may have seen him at the park last night."

"Really? How do you know it was the guy?"

"Oh, Art, have you heard about the terrible fire at Joe Burns's house? That's where I was when the false alarm occurred. Missy helped save Joe's granddaughter."

"Didn't know he had a granddaughter," Art mumbled to himself. "Was anyone hurt badly?"

Alex shook his head. "Thank God. It was a terrible mess though. By the way, it was set."

"Set? How do you know that?"

Irritation strengthened Alex's voice. "Because I examined the remains along with the fireman."

"Well, don't get mad at me! You might think I did it."

"Get serious, Art. Boy, I'd like to get my hands on the guy who did such a needless, awful thing."

"Alex, calm down." Art closed the door to their room. Then he turned back to Alex. "Let's keep a level head here."

When Alex had finished explaining the plan, Art asked, "Do you and Pete have a schedule for our watches at the park?"

Alex shook his head. "Not really."

"Well, how about going to set it up with Pete now?"

"That's a good idea." Then Alex sighed. "I was thinking. Art, it's been awhile since you led one of the fellowship meetings. Do you want to take it next time? That way I can take the first watch, if that's agreeable with you and Pete. I wish I could get ahold of Todd Francis too. I really want to talk to him."

"Sure, I'll lead next meeting. I can do a study on God's Judgment. You tend to emphasize the love and not the wrath."

"Yeah, I know, but people need to understand that they will be accepted by God unconditionally if only they will trust Jesus. Harshness doesn't always work at first. The two need to be properly balanced."

"But," Art persisted, "God always wins—sooner or later—God's Judgment will prevail. What is right must be dutifully upheld. You'll see. Judgment will come." Art declared.

"Easy, Art. You don't want to be too overwhelming."

When they entered the lobby of Stanton House, Alex headed for the stairs to begin the long climb to the fourth floor.

"Hey, Alex," Art called. "Don't you usually check your mail when you come in this way? I think you have something."

Alex went over to check messages as Art had just done, and he found two small slips of memo paper in his mailbox.

"Well, how about that," he exclaimed.

"What now?" Art asked.

"Here I was trying to track down Todd Francis, and I get a message from him that he wants to meet with me tomorrow morning at the coffee shop in the Student Union. Says he'll be there for about an hour and the time." Alex looked up and shoved the paper into his jeans pocket. "Art, I'm going to call

Missy, and then I'll meet you at Pete's room. She's the other message."

"Figures," Art muttered to himself as he took the steps.

Afterward, Alex took the railing and scuffled his feet as he slowly climbed the stairs. His head was beginning to throb. He didn't need another mystery. Didn't he have enough problems to solve? This time he would be ready for Pete's greeting.

"It's about time you got here," Art complained when he opened the door for Alex.

"So what's the news?" Pete didn't disappoint him after all.

"Plenty of news," Alex said as he slumped onto an available chair. "Missy said that she had gone to visit Joe and Ashley in the Iandale Hospital this afternoon..."

"So what?" Art interrupted.

"Joe and Ashley Burns had already been released from the hospital earlier today. She wanted to know if I knew where they had gone to stay." Alex threw up his hands in a gesture of frustration. "How would I know where they went? I haven't been to the hospital since before I took Zoe to report her missing necklace this morning."

"Maybe Mr. McGuire knows where they are staying," Pete speculated. "Funny they didn't leave word though."

"I hope so." Alex folded his arms across his chest. "I certainly would like to know what Todd Francis has on his mind."

"Maybe he is going to make a confession," Art offered.

8

Winter's Loving Chill

Alex arrived at the coffee shop around ten ten the next morning. Amid various round tables and chairs, Alex searched for the bearded man who usually wore a London Fog raincoat. Todd did not disappoint him. A long, tan coat arm waving wildly in the air caught Alex's eye.

"Yes, good morning, Mr. Francis," Alex acknowledged the waving arm and pushed his way through the crowded chairs toward the appropriate table.

Todd gave Alex a friendly smile as he approached the older man. "Help yourself to some muffins and coffee," Todd offered.

"Thank you. I got your message last night, Mr. Francis. I am glad to meet with you. Funny thing is, I was trying to locate you yesterday, and then I got your message."

"Yes, well, I seem to be a bit on the run these days. Let's dispense with the formalities since we'll be working together, in a manner of speaking. Since you're one of the head marshals for the college, I thought I'd better have a chat with you about the Burns family." He handed Alex a business card while he talked.

Alex nodded. "You know where they are? My friend Missy is very concerned about them."

"Yes, well, we thought it best to get them settled without too much commotion, you understand. You know Mr. McGuire, don't you?"

Alex nodded then swallowed his bite of apple muffin. Then he answered, "Yes, Joe's boss, one of the college administrators."

"Mmm. He asked the faculty if anyone knew who could put them up until Joe's house is repaired. Beebee offered to ask her parents, Dennis and Carol Babette. Naturally, they agreed since they live alone and have plenty of room. They own a two-story old colonial on ten wooded acres just outside of town." Todd dipped his bran muffin into the cup of black liquid and proceeded to devour it.

"Who is Beebee?" Alex asked.

"Oh, goodness, let me explain. Beebee is my wife Barbara's nickname from high school, but don't ever call her that to her face." Todd rubbed his cheek with his free hand. "The results could be striking. She got the name for her initials Barbara Babette and for her phobia of bees. She is allergic to their stings, and that's why she hates the name."

"Oh, so your wife's maiden name is Babette. That's why I saw the name in the phone book when I was . . . uh, I was looking for Joe Burns's address."

Todd nodded and held out the plate of muffins to Alex. "We wanted to get the poor chaps settled and then let people know where they are staying, you see? Here, I'll give you the address and directions." Taking a small notebook from his breast pocket, Todd scrawled the information down and handed the paper across to Alex.

"Thanks." Alex put the piece of paper in his shirt pocket and then took another sip of his coffee. "Todd, does your wife know anything about one of her students missing a trinket?"

The older man leaned back in his chair. "I don't recall."

"I thought perhaps she might have mentioned it," Alex persisted. "My friend Missy and her roommate Zoe are in one of her creative writing classes. Zoe thinks someone stole her keepsake. It's a little clay beehive on a gold chain. Apparently one of a kind, so she says."

Todd rose from his chair and picked up his bill. "I really couldn't say, Alex. I must be going though. Nice to chat with you." He turned to leave, and Alex called after him.

"Don't forget your raincoat." Alex passed it to him.

The sultry air seemed to breathe a warning when Alex stepped outside the Student Union building to walk the block and a half to Falcon Hall to leave Missy a message. She would be relieved to know the whereabouts of her new friends. Did he dare to tell her about his feelings though? He shook his head as if to erase his thoughts. When he reached the lobby, he wrote a short note for her to call him at his dorm after four o'clock when he would be finished classes. He had stated that he had good news. After placing the small paper in her mailbox, he left.

He and Art were studying when a light tapping sound rattled the door to their room. Alex strode swiftly over to open it. An exhilarating warmth surged within him as his eyes surveyed his brown-haired, brown-eyed lady dressed in boots, blue jeans, and a bright-red parka. Her smile seemed to be just for him alone.

She was speaking to him. "You said you have good news, Alex? That's a welcome change."

"Missy, come in. I'm glad to see you."

He was still smiling after he had turned to pick up a piece of notebook paper from his desk. He then handed it to her. The names of Joe and Ashley Burns along with an address and phone number stared boldly at her in large letters.

She looked from the paper to Alex. "Thank God they're all right. I've never heard of that street. Alex, how did you find th—"

"If you two are going to have a lengthy conversation," Art interrupted, "please do it somewhere else. I'm trying to do a Bible study lesson here. Thank you."

"Sorry, Art," Alex apologized. "I'll get my jacket, and we can go for a walk before supper. I have some things I want to talk to you about anyway, honey."

"Make sure you put on your winter jacket. The weather forecast is predicting snow, and the sky looks to be in agreement for a change."

"Yeah, I know." Alex slid his arms into his royal-blue parka and pulled on his hood. Reaching out for the red nylon behind her head, he said, "Here I'll fix your hood." His large, warm hands gently trying unsuccessfully to stuff long, brown locks into the sides of the hood brought a jubilant smile to her lips.

"Not like that." She smiled up at him while she pulled down the hood to rearrange her hair.

He went to open the door. They stepped out into the hall, and Alex closed the door quietly. Then they headed for the stairs. As Alex opened the lobby door for her, they both were greeted by a blast of stinging cold air.

"Feels as if it's going to snow." Missy shivered slightly. "Where are we going to walk?"

"This way, honey." Alex put his left arm around her shoulders and eased her body closer to his. "Warmer?"

Her smile reassured him, but she quickly looked away so as not to miss a curbing and to watch where her feet were stepping.

"So tell me, Alex. How did you find out where the Burns are

staying? Do you know how to get there? Are there any clues yet about the fire?"

"Whoa, slow down. I'm sorry, I was thinking... Well, never mind." He went on to explain about his meeting with Todd Francis and the plan that Pete and he had devised. Then he sighed.

She glanced up at him. "Something wrong?"

"No, not exactly. There is something that I want... need... to tell you. I just don't know how to begin."

"Alex, you're my friend. You can talk to me about anything. I can keep a confidence."

Anything? he wondered. Could it really be different this time? Or was he asking too much? What had she said—just friends, nothing more? His gloved hand on her shoulder tightened momentarily. Then he relaxed it to a lighter touch.

Out loud he said, "It can wait. Maybe another time. By the way, you should have seen the look on Todd's face when I mentioned the missing necklace."

"Oh, really?"

"Yeah. After that he was in a hurry to leave. He didn't want to talk about it, not with me anyway."

"That's odd."

He nodded. Then, correcting himself, he agreed verbally.

"I hope it turns up soon." Missy continued, "Zoe is pretty upset about it. She has had more than her share of problems this year, her first year of college too. She had that dream again. Has she told you about it, Alex?"

"I don't think so."

Missy began to explain. "Zoe has a persistent nightmare that keeps recurring. It takes place apparently in a large, old house. In it she is running from something, but she doesn't know why. When she goes downstairs to the kitchen, she sees the ghost of an elderly lady in a rose-colored robe. The woman tells her, 'Do what you must do.' Zoe screams and wakes herself up. I think I would scream too if I dreamed it." Missy concluded.

"That is scary," Alex agreed.

"Alex, where are we anyway? It's dark out, you know."

"I thought I would share my quiet place with you. We're on the county fairgrounds. It's quiet out here this time of year. I like to ride my bike out here when I... when I need to be alone."

Noticing the rigidity in her body, he slipped his arm from her shoulders and stopped walking. He stood facing her.

Missy could feel his warm breath when he whispered her name. She enjoyed the distinctive fragrance of his aftershave. His face was close to hers now.

"Please don't be afraid of me, Missy. I could never hurt you. Trust me."

She parted her lips to speak, but his gentle kiss silenced her words. Inside she felt a warm, aching tenderness. Missy barely had time to breathe when his lips joined with hers again in a long, heart-stopping union.

In the silence that followed, Alex took a step back to remove his gloves and shove them into his pockets. He seemed to be looking right inside her, searching her heart. Warm palms cupped her chin. He rubbed the cold, smooth flesh of her cheeks with warm, caressing fingertips.

When she spoke, her voice trembled. "Alex, I don't think we should be doing this." Inwardly, she was trying to ignore the racing of her heart.

That irresistible, uplifting smile spread across his face. She could hear pleasure in his voice when he spoke. "So you have noticed my feelings for you, fair lady."

"Alex, I love being with you too, but I'm not ready for a commitment yet."

"Say that again, Missy."

"Say what again?"

"That you love being with me." He brushed her lips briefly with his.

"Oh, yes, Alex, you know I do. It just isn't that simple."

"Why not?"

"Alex, please, stop doing that. I can't think straight."

"What am I doing?"

"Touching me that way." She put red-mittened hands over his longer fingers.

Alex dropped his hands away from her face. She heard the swish of nylon as he folded his arms across his chest.

"Don't be afraid of me, Missy. You know I would never hurt you. I am a Christian too. I could never ask you to violate God's commandments, especially in such an important matter as us. I just want to know if you share my feelings at all. Is there any chance for us, sweetheart?"

She sighed. Her boots made a crunching sound in the dirt. "Yes, of course, I do. But why can't we just be close friends?"

"This is why . . ."

She heard the soft sigh as he unlocked his arms. Warm hands on her bare wrists gently pulled her arms forward to encircle him. His arms around her were reassuring, calming, comforting. Then her senses stood still, and her emotions surged in a breathless moment as his kiss said more than words. She could not deny the naturalness of it, the rightness that she had been fighting.

Gently he released her lips but held her body close in warm embrace. He pulled in a long breath of air then released it shakily.

Finally, he said, "Now, Melissa, look at me and tell me you don't care."

"Oh, Alex, you already know more of my feelings for you than I have been willing to admit to myself."

While hugging her closely, Alex prayed softly to himself, "Thank you, Jesus." Then louder, he said to her, "That's all I ask, Missy, is hope for us. Time and hope."

After a few moments of silent embrace, he spoke again.

"Missy, there is one more thing. With Thanksgiving break coming up fast, you'll be going home to Manchester. I won't be that far away in Milford, but it might as well be another state without a driver's license. Missy, I want you to be my steady girl—you and me only."

He felt her body tremble while silent tears stung her eyes. "I . . . I don't know what to say, Alex."

"Say yes, Missy. Say you will."

She pulled herself out of his embrace to calm her emotions.

"Alex, it isn't that simple. Oh, I wish . . . I don't know . . . It's not fair—to you or to me. Alex, I have a double handicap. People usually ignore me. You must know, I've never dated before. I wouldn't know what love is if I fell over it."

"None of that matters. When it is right, you know it. Don't cry, honey. All right, look, at least can we be more than just friends?"

She nodded and took several minutes to calm herself. "Yes, sweetheart, I think we already are."

He had replaced his gloves and now took her hand. "I can accept that for now, Missy. *Hope* is a wonderful word." He placed a quick kiss on her cheek and then said, "Let's start walking back."

Silence followed as they began to retrace their steps.

Finally Missy spoke. "Alex, I know another good word. It's *hunger*."

"Ah." He stopped walking and released her hand. Raising

his arms in the air and making a low growling sound in his throat, he pretended to be getting ready to pounce.

She laughed. "No, tiger, not that kind of hunger. I meant, food hunger. It must be almost six o'clock by now."

"Don't worry, fair lady. We'll make it in time before the dining commons close."

Subtly, gently, light snowflakes began to float downward, hardly noticeable at first as they walked. Silently, Alex thanked the Lord for one recently answered prayer. Another time he would confide in her. He certainly didn't want to risk losing her this early in their relationship. He had just crossed a fragile threshold. Take it one step at a time.

"Alex, I wish I could find some way to help Zoe."

He had to force himself to concentrate on what she was saying. "I'll try to help too, Missy, if I can. By the way, that reminds me, I forgot to tell you that Art is going to lead the next fellowship meeting. Do you think you can persuade Zoe to come?"

"I don't know. I've been praying about it. She wasn't very receptive after the first time she went. I'll try again. She is so afraid to trust anyone with her feelings."

"Mmm hmm."

She heard nylon slide as his head nodded. Her heart skipped a beat as his gloved hand released hers and came around her waist.

"Well, no one likes a broken heart," she said.

His arm tightened around her waist. "Missy, you'll probably think I'm crazy. I have a terrible feeling that someone is going to try to hurt you somehow. I can't explain it, but it's there. It's an unmistakable fearful feeling."

"You are probably worrying about the bomb threats. That is enough to rattle anyone. Hopefully the person doing it will be caught soon."

"You know Pete, Art, and I have a plan there."

"You be careful, Alex. Criminology is for the police lab and not the school fire marshals and newspaperman."

"I don't like it, Missy. This situation has to be stopped."

"That's for sure," she agreed. "It's getting too cold outside at night anyway to be standing around on the front lawn of a dormitory in night clothes."

Alex chuckled softly as he allowed his mind to wander.

"Aha, it's snowing! I can feel it," Missy exclaimed with childlike excitement.

"Mmm hmm. I hope there is something warm for supper."

"Alex, I have to study tonight. Will you walk me back to the dorm after supper?"

"Of course. Speaking of studying, did you get your information on Ashley for your case study?"

"Oh, yes. She is a beautiful young lady. Although she is somewhat troubled, she is a Christian believer. May I ask whom you chose for your report?"

"Oh, I'll rope my younger brother into doing it over Thanksgiving break."

"You're lucky to have a brother. I don't have one or a sister."

"Well, now you have me." Under the light from an overhead streetlamp, he could see moisture gleaming her eyes. "Missy, are you okay?"

She nodded. They kept walking. Alex could see the familiar grounds of the gymnasium in the distance, and he knew they would soon reach the Iandale State College campus.

This day of first snow marked a beginning to first mature love.

9

Approaching Judgment

"Missy, I don't know why I let you and the guys talk me into going to your Christian meeting again. I am getting another migraine too."

"Maybe you'll feel better once we get outside. Besides, Zo, I've noticed your interest in Art."

"Oh, you have, huh? Well, at least you aren't denying your interest in Alex lately. They'll be here pretty soon to pick us up. Hmp. They don't even trust me to get there on my own." Zoe sat down at her desk.

"Zoe, that's it. Trust. That is what is really bothering you. For salvation from sin and death, you have to put your complete trust in Jesus Christ. You must trust Him with your life, Zoe. Don't let fear or doubt keep you from taking that first step of faith. Trust in the Lord with all your heart. Jesus will never leave you nor forsake you." Missy leaned against the wall. "As for the guys picking us up here, they are being extra nice, or extra careful. It's been awhile since we've had a b—"

"Don't say it!" Zoe interrupted sharply. "Just don't say any more. Here, let me fix your collar, Missy."

Missy got up and walked over to where Zoe was sitting.

"You don't usually wear a dress," Zoe continued. "Why tonight?"

Missy straightened and shrugged her shoulders. "Art isn't as easygoing as Alex. I thought I'd look a little more formal. I know. I usually only wear dresses to church. Art makes me feel uneasy sometimes, as if I really don't belong," Missy confessed.

A loud knocking on their door startled both girls. Missy, in boots, padded quickly over to open it. Her smile weakened quickly with Art's impatience.

"Hurry up and get your coats," he snapped.

Missy obeyed and took her parka from Zoe.

Zoe smiled. "It's nice to see you too, Art."

Alex was beside Missy now, and she slipped her hand around his puffy blue sleeve. His gentle voice always reassured her. "Don't mind him. Art's just nervous."

Art made a dismissing gesture with his hand.

Zoe slammed the door and locked it behind them. "He's not the only one who's nervous."

"Relax, Zoe," Art tried to reassure her. He held out an arm for her to join him. It encircled her waist, and she matched stride with him as they headed for the stairs.

"Thanks, Alex," Missy said.

"For what?"

"For being you."

His kiss held aching sweetness.

"Mmm. Are you sure you want to go to this meeting?" he asked.

She giggled joyfully and tugged at his arm. "We'd better."

Art opened the meeting with prayer and then the songs "A Closer Walk" and "Trust and Obey." Then he began his message.

"Mark my words, people. The day of God's wrath is coming. There is an approaching Judgment. Right now, God is holding back, so to speak. He is patiently waiting for those of us who will accept His plan of salvation in Jesus Christ to come forward and be counted righteous. Once this is accomplished, His wrath will prevail. Look at it in your Bibles. Turn with me to Romans chapter 2 and verse 5." He read, "But because of your stubbornness and unrepentant heart, you are storing up wrath for yourself in the day of wrath and revelation of the righteous judgment of God." Then he looked up and concluded, "You see, judgment will prevail."

Pausing for a moment, Art stood and placed his Bible down gently on his chair. He began to walk slowly around inside the gathered circle of chairs.

"So you see, those of us who have made a choice to follow Jesus in our daily lives have an obligation. God loves us, but He hates sin. Therefore, it is our duty to stand up for the cause of righteousness. According to 1 John 1:9, it is our duty to cleanse the world from all unrighteousness."

"Missy, where is that reference?" Zoe whispered.

Missy took the Bible that Zoe held out to her and used her magnifying glass to find the verse that Art had just misinterpreted. She handed the book back to Zoe and shook her head slightly.

Art picked up his Bible, closed it with a thump, and sat down again. He was about to close his lecture. "It is really very simple," he concluded. "We can either accept God's gift of salvation through Christ now or face God's judgment for the unbeliever in the Day of Wrath. It is also called Jacob's Trouble and the Great Tribulation. Just remember that 'every knee will bow and every tongue will swear allegiance.' Need I say more? Thanks. Good night." Art rose to leave.

Alex stood to offer a time of prayer for those who wished to remain longer.

To Missy's surprise, Zoe's cold and trembling hand reached out for hers. "Missy, I think I want to try it God's way."

Missy squeezed Zoe's hand. She could not see the lack of color in her friend's face. She motioned for Alex to join them, and she was surprised at the tremor in her own voice. "Alex will lead you in prayer, Zoe."

Alex came to stand behind the blond and place his hands on her shoulders. His steady voice instilled a soothing calmness as he instructed Zoe to repeat his words.

Zoe was sobbing openly now in between phrases. Missy still held her hand as she prayed silently along with Pete and Laurie who had also stayed. At the close of her prayer, Zoe received Missy's hug gratefully.

"You'll never regret that decision, Zoe." Pete gave her a warm smile. "Believe me."

"God bless you, Zoe." Alex gave her shoulders a squeeze then released them. "We have been praying for you."

Zoe looked up into Laurie's quivering smile and tearstained cheeks.

"Feeling better?" Alex asked her.

Zoe sighed then nodded. A faint smile relaxed her face.

"It's about time something good happened to you, Zo." Missy's heart soared. She wondered to herself how it was possible to be this happy. Her newest friend was now an added member to the kingdom of heaven. She thanked the Lord silently. Her fruitful relationship with Alex was more than she had ever dreamed possible.

"Missy, stop daydreaming and put your coat on."

Alex's rousing tone startled her from her thoughts. Although she couldn't see the sparkle in his eyes, his smile told her that he wasn't annoyed. She obediently stood to slide her arms into the sleeves, and he pulled the parka up around her shoulders. When they were ready to leave, she took his arm.

"Zoe, want an arm home?" he offered.

She grinned and stepped to his right side.

Pete teased, "Is that anything like a lift home?" He turned to Laurie, bowed gallantly, and then straightened. "May I walk you back to your dorm?"

"I thought you'd never ask," Laurie replied dramatically. She stepped close to him, and they followed the other three out.

Outside the little group strolled leisurely, treasuring the pleasant circumstances and enjoying one another's comfortable companionship. The brisk evening air stimulated the senses.

"Hey, my headache is gone. Boy, that's a relief," Zoe exclaimed as if she had just realized it.

"What a nice evening," Laurie observed.

"Good old New England winter," Pete said.

"Let's cross here," Alex suggested. "I don't see anything coming."

When the group had stepped off the curb to cross the T-shaped intersection, brakes from an approaching vehicle screeched as it sped up the leg of the T. The oncoming vehicle almost forgot to turn. Seemingly making a split-second decision at the last possible moment, it swerved into the path of the stunned pedestrians. Missy could have reached out and touched the momentary obstruction as it whooshed past, barely missing her, as it swayed to right itself from its abrupt turn.

After checking his left again, Alex paced the distance swiftly, with the two girls in tow, toward the safety of the opposite sidewalk. "Is everyone all right?"

"Yes, Alex." Missy gripped his arm tighter.

Zoe released his other arm to clasp her hands together and

stare wide-eyed at the now-empty street.

"What kind of a nut would drive like that? I don't think the driver ever saw us . . . until, well, almost too late."

"Pete, did you catch the license number? It came on us so fast that I didn't. I . . . I didn't even see it coming . . ." Alex let his voice trail off.

"No, I didn't either. It came too suddenly to react. I know it was a station wagon though. Dark color, I think."

"That's something to go on," Laurie added.

"Sure is. Thanks, Laurie. Well, let's get going. We still have to get you girls back to the dorm, and we have one more street to cross," Pete reminded them.

"Peter!" Laurie admonished.

The others started ahead, but Missy held back. She noticed that Alex's arm was trembling.

"Alex, are you okay?"

No reaction.

"Alex, what's wrong?"

He did not speak or move, except that his arm continued to shake.

After a few moments, his arm fell still. Realization seized her. Again, with new understanding, she tried to rouse him from his state. She removed one mitten to touch his face.

"Alex?"

"Huh? What?"

"Alex, it's all right. I understand." She took her hand away.

"No, you don't," he mumbled. Then he said, "It's just nerves."

She almost tripped as he abruptly started walking to catch up with the others.

"Hey, no lovey-dovey stuff, you two." Pete threw the jib over his shoulder.

"We weren't," Alex snapped.

"You look a little pale, Alex," Zoe observed.

"I expect we all do," he answered quickly. "I had to take a minute to calm down after that scare."

They crossed the remaining street without incident.

"Good night, guys, and thanks," Zoe said and then went inside.

"May I escort you again?" Pete asked Laurie as he followed her into the lobby.

"Alex, I want to tell you that I . . ."

"Missy," he interrupted, "just don't say any more. I'm tired, and you must be too."

She reached for his hand. "Well, don't be upset. It is over and done with. No one could have anticipated that maniac driver coming at us."

"Yeah, I know. Now get inside."

"Don't I even get a good night kiss?" She squeezed his hand.

"Oh." His lips brushed hers all too briefly.

She released his hand and turned to go inside just as Pete was coming out. He held the door for her.

"Shall we head back to our lonely rooms, Pete?"

"Seriously, Alex," Pete said as they began to walk, "that's the first time I've gotten Laurie's attention, and the night had to end like this."

"Oh? You didn't tell me. I could ask Missy to put in some good words with her for you," Alex teased.

"No, now wait a minute. I can handle myself, like you."

They had almost reached the street when Pete noticed it. The bushes around the dorm whispered their protests, and twigs and branches snapped their disapproval as they were forced into movement by a large unseen figure.

Pete raised a hand for Alex to stop.

"There is someone or something in the bushes back there. I heard it."

Pete turned and moved quickly and quietly followed closely by Alex. The rustle of the bushes told them that the thing was escaping behind the dorm.

Alex stopped and raised a cautioning hand. "Pete, we'll never catch it. We don't have lights or weapons."

Pete slapped his knee. "I know something moved back there, Alex. I heard it."

"Yeah, I know. I heard it too. It could have been an animal," Alex suggested dubiously.

"Too big, I think," Pete replied. "But let's go. We don't need to be caught snooping around back here ourselves."

"That's for sure," Alex agreed. To himself he said, *Now we are both frustrated, but for different reasons.*

10

The Final Test

Melissa found it hard to realize that a week had already passed since Thanksgiving break. She stood in front of her closet, trying to decide what to change into for her visit to the Babette's home. She was grateful for Dr. and Mr. Francis's offer to drive her and Alex out there. Missy was looking forward to seeing Joe and Ashley Burns again. She hadn't had much time to talk with Joe on campus since the fire. The thought of home cooking, since Carol Babette had invited them to stay for supper, was an added delight to her anticipation.

Searching through her clothes, she pulled out a rose-patterned blouse. As she turned to lay it on the bed, Missy ran her free hand down its slippery, smooth synthetic surface.

"Mmm."

The texture of the material reminded her of the smooth coolness of ice cream. Turning back to the closet to choose a skirt, she realized that she didn't even know Alex's favorite color. Frowning a little, Missy wondered if she could successfully manage seeing more of Alex and keeping up with her studies too. Final exams were less than two weeks away. Another semester would be finished. She fervently wished the police's success in capturing the person making the disgusting phone calls and bomb threats.

Why is it taking them so long to figure it out? she wondered.

After pulling out a matching skirt for the blouse and a beige button-down sweater, she closed the closet door.

When she had finished changing, Missy made a face at herself in the mirror above her bureau. Alex would be picking her up soon to meet the Francis's at Parker House.

As Alex and Melissa approached the building, he led her around to the parking lot behind Parker House. In the lot stood a lonely dark-gray station wagon.

"It certainly won't be hard to tell which car is theirs," Missy observed. "That is Dr. Francis's station wagon."

"Here comes Todd now." Alex told her.

Todd Francis smiled and then greeted them. The two men shook hands.

"And this must be your charming friend Melissa. I'm delighted to finally meet you, my dear. Alex didn't tell me how pretty you really are." Todd kissed her hand.

"Thank you, Mr. Francis." Missy flushed at his politeness.

"Please call me Todd Melissa. Barbara is a bit more formal than I, you understand. I should warn you, she isn't quite herself these days. You'll like her parents, however. Decent chaps."

"Then your Thanksgiving trip to England didn't help her mood? She told us about it in class," Missy explained.

Todd frowned and shook his head. "I'm afraid not. Won't you two come inside while she finishes up her paperwork? The sun may be warm, but the air is quite nippy in December."

They followed him inside Parker House and waited in the hall while Barbara Francis was preparing her final exam for her

English classes. Her husband went back into her office.

"That was really nice of the Babettes to invite us to Sunday night supper," Missy commented. "Have you met them yet?"

"No, but Todd has told me about them. They will probably welcome company. They both are retired, and they live in a large house all by themselves. I wonder if I will want a lot of company when I am old enough to be retired."

"Hmm." Melissa wore a puzzled expression. She thought for a moment before replying. "I don't think you have to start worrying about it now. Haven't you heard? You're as young as you feel."

"I know. That's what worries me."

"I really haven't thought that far ahead yet," Missy admitted. "Joe Burns certainly isn't worrying about his age. But I wish I could do something to help his aching heart. Alex? Are you listening? You seem to be somewhere else." Missy reached up with her left hand to touch his cheek. It felt cold from the chill of winter.

At the warmth of her touch, he blinked and looked down into her face. She could not see the deep, searching gaze he gave her.

"Sweet Melissa." He breathed the words softly. "Why does life have to be complicated by problems? Why can't it just be simple?"

"Only God knows all the answers. We just have to trust Him and grow in His strength."

He took her face in his hands, holding it gently. "I love being with you." His kiss told her this and more.

"I'm glad we have this day to share, Alex," she whispered.

"Lord willing, I hope there—" Alex paused in midsentence. "Missy, did you hear that? It sounded like a car door slamming."

"No, Alex. I can't hear that in here."

"Oh, yeah, that's right." He left her embrace to walk across the hall to look out the window overlooking the parking lot. There was no sign of movement. "Hmp. I don't see anything." He returned to stand beside Missy.

She said, "I hope Dr. Francis isn't going to be much longer. I'm anxious to see Ashley again."

"Oh. Don't you like being alone with me?"

She grinned. "Of course I do. Alex, you know what I mean..."

"Missy, you know I have one more year of school after this and you have two." Alex hesitated for a minute then continued. "Missy, I wish we could spend them together—I mean, all the time."

"Alex, I don't know if I can handle studying for a career and having a serious dating relationship too. I've been doing a lot of thinking about it, and I don't know how it will all work out. I want to be honest with you. I love you, but I have to be realistic."

"What? Say that again."

"What do you mean? Say what again?" she repeated.

"You said that you love me, Missy."

"Yes—I mean, I love being with you, Alex. I... I... love you as a dear Christian fr—"

His warm kiss silenced her words.

"Now, am I still just your friend?" Not giving her time to answer, he pressed his lips to hers again.

For a long moment afterward, Missy gazed into his face. Her lips were parted as if she were pouring out her heart's confusion. Missy could not see the warmth and tenderness that his blue eyes held for her.

She drew a deep breath to speak. "Alex, I... I wish you wouldn't kiss me so... so... like that... You mess up my thinking. One minute I'm telling you I don't know if it will work between us and the next . . ." She dropped her head to look at the floor. "My body aches to hold you. I dread Christmas break because we will be separated for three weeks."

Alex pulled her close, enfolding her in his arms. His parka felt cold against her cheek as she rested her head against him. He rested his chin lightly on top of her head. For a long moment, they held each other tightly, resting in the growing strength of their deepening commitment.

Finally, Alex drew back slightly. Missy looked up. "Missy." He cleared his throat. "There is something I need to talk to you about. I haven't had the courage before now, but there is something you have to know."

"Darling, you can tell me anything. I do love you, Alex."

He hugged her again. When he became aware of footsteps approaching, he breathed a long sigh. "They're coming, Missy."

"Who?"

"The Francises. Remember?"

"Oh."

"Sorry to keep you waiting."

Barbara Francis's voice was calm enough, but Alex noticed a pallor to her face and redness around her green eyes. He also saw that she was holding tightly to her husband's arm. Alex offered his arm to Missy, who eagerly fell into stride with him as they followed the older couple outside. As they approached the lone car, Barbara spoke to her husband.

"Todd, darling, would you open the back? I'll put my briefcase in there. Do you have your keys?"

Nodding in reply, her husband reached into his pocket. She also had a set of keys to his jeep in case of an emergency. Todd tried his key in the lock. It clicked, but the door would not open.

"It appears to be stuck."

He pulled harder on the handle. Next he removed then

replaced the key to try again.

"Did you see that?" Barbara asked emphatically.

"See what, love?" her husband asked.

"Oh." She hesitated. "Uh, nothing . . . I guess. Well, I thought . . . I thought I saw the car blanket in the corner move. My eyes must have been playing tricks."

By this time, Todd had gotten the lock opened and gone around to open the side doors for Alex and Missy. Barbara dropped the briefcase hastily on top of the blanket and continued to stare at it. While she alone watched, the briefcase appeared to tilt to one side then heave slightly in the opposite direction and slip to rest on the carpeting.

Barbara walked quickly to the front passenger side of her station wagon and climbed inside. "Let's get going, Todd." She slammed the door shut with a decisive jolt.

Upon adjusting the seat to his length, Todd got in on the driver's side. He glanced over his shoulder at Alex and Missy huddled together on the passenger side in the back seat.

"I guess we're all set," Alex said.

Alex saw Todd's smile as his head turned back to face front and start the car. Todd eased the wagon out of its parking space and headed in the direction of the fairgrounds toward the outskirts of the town of Iandale.

"Alex, you were going to tell me something important," Missy prompted as they rode.

"Oh, uh, it can wait until another time, honey. I just want to enjoy this day with you. Dr. Francis, do you often work in your office on weekends?"

The woman turned to look at Alex and smiled wryly. "Finals are as much work for the teacher as they are for the students. We have to come up with the brilliant questions in the first place. But I must admit that I don't enjoy being alone on campus this semester. That's why I asked my husband to come to the office with me."

"I don't blame you," Missy agreed.

"Why does it bother you that much, Dr. Francis?" Alex persisted.

"One night last month I stayed late to work in my office, and I became frightened by noises. I just knew there was someone else in the building. I kept hearing scraping sounds as if furniture was being moved and then slow footsteps and heavy breathing, but I couldn't see anyone. Finally, I became so uncomfortable that I got out of there as quickly as I could. I couldn't wait to get home. I don't like driving at night anyway, especially in the winter. Since that awful night, I have not stayed alone after daytime hours. You understand?"

"Of course. You're right, Doctor," Missy encouraged her. "Tell me, how is Ashley? I am so looking forward to seeing her again. Did she find it hard adjusting after the fire?"

"She is fine. I think that moving out here with my folks has been excellent therapy for all of them, especially Joe." This time her smile was warm and amiable. "My parents are very loving and supportive people. I don't know what I would have done without them when I was . . . uh, that is, during my high school years." She turned back to face front and watch the view.

"My high school years weren't all that great either," Missy admitted. "I would have been lost without my family too."

"There have been days that I would have gladly written off the calendar," Alex confessed.

"I'm sure we all can say that," Todd said. Then he added, "By the way, we have video of our trip to see my family in Yorkshire, England, if you chaps would like to see them."

Both Alex and Missy were enthusiastic in their agreement.

In a short time they had reached their destination. They

were greeted at the door by Carol Babette, Barbara's mother.

Alex and Missy were ushered into a large open entranceway. Missy noticed the high ceiling and long ivory-colored arch above them. The deep-rose color in the carpet also caught her eye.

"Come into the living room, won't you? Ashley is excited about your visit, and we are glad to have you." Carol smiled and gestured toward a doorway to their left.

As the party entered the room, Dennis Babette and Joe Burns stood in greeting. To Missy's surprise, Ashley jumped up from her spot on the floor in front of the fireplace to run to meet her with a wonderful hug.

"I missed you, Missy. Happy Christmas."

"Happy Christmas to you too, sweetie," Missy replied. "I have been wanting to come to see you."

"I hope you saved a hug for me too, Ashley. I like to hug pretty ladies," Alex said then smiled.

Ashley looked to her grandfather, who nodded, and then said, "Okay, Alex."

When Ashley reached out, Alex picked her up and twirled her around while holding on to her tightly. Ashley's delighted giggles filled the room with the music of laughter. Then Alex set her down gently and held onto her for a moment, making sure that Ashley had regained her balance before he let go of her arms.

"That's a very pretty dress, Ashley. Red is my favorite color," he told her. Alex smiled down at the young girl.

Missy made a mental note.

Ashley was tugging on her hand. "Missy, can you see the tree? Isn't it pretty? Come closer."

Missy nodded and smiled at her excitement. She could see the triangle-shaped outline of the tall tree. The ornaments and lights looked like small colored dots amid splotches of white and gold against a green background.

Missy's heart leaped as Alex's arm encircled her waist. She knew the pleasant mild scent of his aftershave now enhanced by the added spice of his cologne. She relaxed in the warmth of his closeness and the assurance of his attentiveness. When she looked up at him, she could not see the hint of moisture glistening in his eyes.

"Can you see the angel way up on top of the tree, darling?"

Missy shook her head no, and he described it in detail for her.

"Alex. Look. Look up. See?" Ashley was pointing to the mistletoe hanging from the high ceiling in front of the tree.

"Oh, yes, Ashley, we will have to do something about that."

"What is it?" Missy asked.

Alex drew her to him, hugging her, and caressing her lips with his. He leaned close to her ear to whisper into it. "You smell delicious. We are standing under the mistletoe."

Missy shivered a little as his breath tickled through her hearing aid.

"Missy, can I have a turn now?" Ashley asked. "I want Grandpa to kiss me under the mistletoe."

Joe Burns proudly complied while Alex and Missy went to sit down together.

"That's got to be the biggest tree I've ever seen," Ashley announced. "This is the best Christmas ever. Since my—" Sullenness crept into her bubbly mood. "I didn't mean to forget about Mommy and Daddy, Grandpa. I'm sorry."

"It's all right, sunshine," her Grandpa tried to reassure her.

Sensing her confusion, Missy tried to explain. "Ashley, you needn't feel guilty about having fun. Your parents loved you very much, and they would want you to enjoy the holidays.

Remembering good times with your parents makes you happy. But then you are sad because you miss them, right?"

Ashley nodded.

"Don't be afraid to let your true feelings show themselves. Ashley, when you share your hurts, God can work to help heal them. Your parents wouldn't want you to feel guilty for being happy. Your happiness was important to them as it is to your Grandpa. Cherish your memories, Ashley, but don't let them steal your future. Love keeps no record of wrongs."

Privately, Alex recalled Missy's biblical reference.

"Ashley, she's right," Joe confessed. "For years I felt angry about the car accident. I couldn't see beyond the loss. That is, until this young lady helped to open my eyes. Don't be afraid to talk about how you feel. Do you understand, sunshine?"

Ashley nodded.

"Excuse me." Barbara stood and walked quickly out of the room.

"Let her go, Carol," Todd spoke quietly to his mother-in-law as she rose to follow her daughter. "You know that she has to work this out for herself."

"It is much easier to give advice than to take it," Alex observed wisely, "especially when it's your own."

Todd nodded his agreement.

"Missy?"

"Yes, Ashley?"

"Would you want to go outside with me and make a snowman? I don't have anyone to play with."

"You bet I would. But no rough stuff in this skirt, okay?"

"Deal." Ashley beamed.

They had been outside for over an hour when Ashley came bounding back into the living room. Politely she asked to borrow some buttons and a scarf for their new snowman, which

Missy had promised to watch while she went to fetch the treasures. Clutching her trinkets, Ashley ran back outside after thanking Auntie Carol.

Seconds later, the steel door banged again, and Ashley came running into the room, screaming in hysterics.

"Alex, Uncle Todd, Grandpa . . . you gotta come help Missy! There's a man fighting with her on the ground! Come on! Hurry!"

Joe grabbed Ashley by the arm and held her firmly. "Ashley, you stay here with us and let the men handle this."

Dennis Babette quickly went to the kitchen phone to call the police. Alex and Todd dashed for the door in shirt sleeves.

Missy lay on her back in the snow. She was pinned to the ground by a large male figure who was now thrusting her legs apart and tearing into her defenseless nylon stockings with his fingernails. He had gagged her mouth with a wrinkled and dirty scarf from his pocket. Missy's attempts at struggling were futile. His broad shoulders held her arms in check. The slight kicks that her boots managed to twist into his long legs did nothing to deter him. His prickly brown beard irritated her face, and the heavy stench of liquor on his breath sickened her heart. Missy was caught with no way out.

A wave of relief swept over Missy as Alex and Todd manhandled and lifted the burdening body off of her. The man didn't seem to be aware of his circumstances because he offered little resistance.

Missy sat up and began to cry as relief gave way to shame and embarrassment. She began to feel around in the snow.

"Go inside, Missy," Todd commanded. "We'll wait for the police out here."

She protested between sobs. "But I've lost a hearing aid."

"Go inside, Missy. We'll find it after," Alex spoke clearly and firmly.

After assuring Ashley that Missy was all right, Barbara took her upstairs to shower and clean up. The patchwork carpeting on the spiral steps felt warm and reassuring under Missy's bare feet.

"That man... he tried to... to..."

"I know," Barbara whispered. "But he didn't succeed, did he?"

Missy shook her head. "If Alex and Todd hadn't come... I... I c-couldn't stop him... I couldn't move. When I first saw him walking toward me, I thought he was Todd. Then he knocked me down and..." Her voice trailed off. She shivered under the rose-colored robe that Barbara had given her.

"You'll feel a little better after a shower, Missy," Barbara lied. "It wasn't your fault. Remember that."

Barbara paced the floor in her old bedroom while Missy was in the shower. She had never confided in anyone except Todd, besides her own parents' knowledge of the incident in her life. Perhaps it would help both of them if she talked to Missy.

When Missy returned, she was toweling her long, brown hair. "Thank you, Dr. Francis. I've never had an experience like that before."

"Missy, you may use my first name outside of class. There is something I would like to tell you. Come, sit down." When they were both seated on the bedside, Barbara began her story.

"You see," she paused and took a deep breath, "when I was only fifteen... I was raped, and I have never quite gotten over it."

Missy burst into tears again and hugged the older woman. Barbara also cried with her, allowing her own hurt and guilt to surface once again. Finally, when they had quieted, Barbara began to confess her feelings.

"I felt so . . . estranged . . . after the incident . . . and the pregnancy. At that young age, I just couldn't see myself raising a daughter even though my parents had offered to adopt her. My grandmother had always told me to do what I must do—that is, do what I felt was right. I have always felt guilty for putting my daughter up for adoption, but I believed that I was too young for that kind of responsibility." She sighed shakily.

"Oh, Barbara, you can't blame yourself. Let go of the guilt," Missy exclaimed.

"There is something else, Missy." Then Barbara sobbed bitterly.

Missy hugged her again. While stroking her back soothingly, she tried to comfort Barbara's aching, agonized heart. "Cast all your cares upon Him, Barbara, because He cares for you. Let go and let God heal."

Barbara's voice faltered as she spoke. "Missy, I think your roommate Zoe Babette is my daughter."

The two women continued to embrace each other for a time. Finally, they regained composure, each drawing strength from the other.

"Thank you, Missy. Somehow I feel relieved. You know you will have to talk to the police downstairs. I'll go and see if your clothes are dry now."

Missy nodded. Silently, she was praying for Barbara and Zoe.

"The police already took the man away," Dennis told the two women after Missy had given her preliminary statement to the policeman who had questioned her.

Alex stood and started to walk toward Missy as she reentered the living room. Instinctively, she took a step backward.

"Please, just don't touch me, Alex. I'm all right."

"Missy? Well then, here. I have your hearing aid." He held his hand open for her to see the small object in it.

"Oh, bless you, Alex." She took the object from his outstretched hand and placed it in her left ear. "Thank you and Todd. If you hadn't come out . . . I . . . I don't even want to think of the consequences. I'm all right though. I just feel kind of creepy. I need a little time to get over this, Alex."

From the kitchen across the wide hall, Ashley came in to announce that supper was being served. Obediently, the adults rose to follow her into the large kitchen. Barbara, while taking her husband's arm, said something to him quietly. He patted her hand in response as they followed Ashley's lead. Joe and Dennis followed them.

"Go ahead, Alex," Missy gestured.

She followed Alex as she tried to put the day's events out of her mind and look forward to a pleasant evening. Maybe now the college campus would be safe again.

11

All Things New

Second semester had already begun. Where had Christmas break gone? A new year had arrived and, hopefully, a new start. Missy and Zoe had enjoyed Christmas vacation in Manchester at Missy's parents' house. Now they found themselves once again in the college bookstore, arming themselves for their new courses of study.

Laurie smiled as Missy and Zoe plunked two stacks of books down on the counter in front of her.

"Is that it for now?" she asked.

"Isn't that enough?" Zoe asked.

Laurie began to ring up the items. "If you two can wait a few minutes for me, I'll be through work and I can walk back to Falcon Hall with you. I have my own stack of books to take."

"Sure," Missy agreed.

"I'll just put yours back here with mine until we're ready." Laurie began to remove the texts while Missy and Zoe continued to browse.

"What we need is some nice guy to come along and carry

those things for us," Zoe commented to her roommate. "Know any?"

"Hmm." Missy smiled. "I might."

"Oh," Zoe remembered, "I better get some more notebook paper while I'm here. You need anything else, Missy?"

"Yeah, blank cassettes for my tape recorder, now that you mentioned it. Now, let's see, where are they?"

"Over there, past the jewelry. Come on, I'll show you," Zoe offered.

"They keep rearranging things," Missy complained.

As they passed the jewelry counter, Zoe sighed. "Gee, Missy. I don't expect that I'll ever get my locket back now. Too bad. I really liked it a lot. I don't think it's worth much money though."

"I don't know, Zo. Ouch! Who's pulling my hair?"

Missy turned to see a tall masculine blond and a shorter redhead with numerous facial freckles both smiling innocently at her.

"Aw, we didn't pull it that hard," Alex teased. "Missy, I've been trying to catch up with you since registration yesterday. I really missed you."

The sincerity in his voice filled her with warmth. "I missed you too, Alex. It has been a long three weeks in that respect. Pete, how are you?"

"Still nosing around," Pete answered cheerfully. "If you folks will excuse me, I want to see Laurie." He turned to walk back through the aisle.

"Good luck, Pete," Alex called.

"Oh?" Zoe nodded wisely.

"Yeah," Alex explained unnecessarily. "He's been trying to get her attention since last semester. Some guys aren't so fortunate." He cleared his throat with exaggeration.

Zoe looked from Alex to Missy. "Should I leave you two alone?"

Missy protested, "No, don't be silly. Besides, we have a load of books to carry. Remember?"

"Want some help?" Alex was eager to offer.

"We thought you'd never ask," Zoe replied. "By the way, Alex, where is Art?"

Zoe saw Alex's expression sober. "He's been keeping to himself since he got back from vacation. Something must have happened, but I don't know what. I guess he isn't ready to talk yet."

"That's too bad," Missy said with concern in her voice.

"Come on, girls," Alex urged. "I see that Laurie is ready. She is motioning for us to follow her. Guess she showed Pete where your books were stashed."

"We'll just pay for these and be right with you," Zoe told him, referring to the small items that she and Missy had gotten.

With the help of Alex and Pete, the load was easier to manage.

"It's great to be back to a normal routine after last semester," Laurie commented as they walked. "I'm glad we don't have to worry about bomb threats anymore."

Pete said, "That guy really didn't know what he was doing to admit that he was the one making those phone calls to the girls' dorms and scaring the girls."

"How in the world did he get way out to Dr. Francis's parents' house in the suburbs anyway?" Laurie asked. "I never did hear the whole story."

Alex explained, "He must have hidden in the back of Dr. Francis's station wagon the afternoon that she and her husband drove Missy and me out there. Hers was the only car in the parking lot at Parker House that day. You know, it's weird. I remember thinking that I heard a door slam while Missy and I were waiting for them inside. I'll bet that he was the one who had frightened Dr. Francis that night too. You remember? The night she almost ran us down when we were crossing the street."

"Well, it's a big relief to have all of that over with," Zoe asserted. Then she asked, "Did he admit to starting the fires too?"

"Nope," Pete answered. "But for someone as spaced out as this guy must have been, I wouldn't have put it past him. He must have done that too. Probably he doesn't even remember."

Missy asked, "What will happen to that man now?"

Alex told her that he had been recommitted to the state hospital for psychiatric treatment and would probably be there for a long time.

"I hope so," Zoe said flatly.

"We should still pray for him," Missy insisted.

"Gosh, Missy, I don't think I would be so generous if I were in your place," Laurie admitted honestly.

Pete raised an eyebrow then commented, "I bet you would."

The group had reached Falcon Hall and begun to climb the two flights of stairs to the third floor. Alex, who was carrying a fair stack of books, took the steps two at a time and waited on the landing for the others.

"Phew. It makes a difference carrying a load of books," Laurie, who was the shortest of the group, complained.

"No kidding," Zoe agreed. "Well, one more flight."

"I'm glad you girls all live on the same floor," Pete said.

"Ah, we made it." Missy felt for the key hole to unlock the room door. "Come on in." She laid her few thick books and bag of accessories on her desk and sat sideways in her chair.

"I'll help Laurie with hers," Pete offered. "See ya."

Zoe smiled as she sat down in front of her desk and deposited her stack.

Missy smiled up at Alex and expressed her thanks as he stepped between the two girls to add his taller stack to the collection.

He, in turn, touched her hand briefly and said warmly, "Anytime, fair lady." Then he too sank into a nearby chair and, clasping his hands behind his head, stretched out his long legs across the floor.

Missy filed away for future recall the mental picture of Alex relaxing in the chair near her. She drew security and confidence from his presence. Her treasured memory would help her to slip back easily into the routine of classes, more assured of a less-stressful semester.

The days began to pass like the steady ticking of a clock.

It was a cold night in mid-January when Alex woke his roommate from a nightmare.

Art sat up breathing heavily at first. He wiped the perspiration from his face with both hands and sighed. After a moment, he was able to speak.

"Thanks, Alex. I just relived my mother's death."

"What? But you went home to spend Christmas break with her."

Art nodded. "Ya, and she died from a massive heart attack two days after Christmas." He blinked back the tears that were threatening to burn his eyes. "She was all I had, Alex. I never knew a father. We were on welfare. I never had much like the other kids did when I was growing up. My Ma always said that I should be thankful for whatever I got. When she got work after I started school, she worked hard and saved everything. I never knew she had a heart condition, Alex." He shook his head. "She never told me. She wasn't very realistic either. 'Look at it for the best,' she used to say. She was always so . . . so . . . cheerful. She made me go to church with her too, and boy, I hated it. I swore to myself that I'd never go to church when I got out on my own. Then in my senior year of high school when I . . . well, I mean, I . . . Alex, I'm sorry. I don't know what I'm saying." Art covered his face with both hands.

"Hey, Art, this is strictly between you and me." Alex touched his roommate lightly on the shoulder and waited. He listened patiently while Art began to release the grief and bitterness he had been holding inside longer than anyone else knew.

Finally, Art shook his head and told him, "I don't think I ever told her that I loved her. I was too busy fighting against her rules."

It was Alex's turn to sigh. He was remembering how hard it was for his family to adjust when his own mother had passed on.

"Moms sense those things, Art. Believe me, they know. We may have many unanswered questions when we arrive in heaven. There isn't much I can say, Art. I don't have any easy answers. But you know that you have hope in Jesus Christ."

"Ya, I know." Art sighed again and dropped his hands to the blanket. Between long, slender fingers, he squeezed its fuzzy blue texture. "It's over anyway. I've got to look ahead, not back. Thanks, buddy. I'm all right now."

"Okay, Art, but if you ever need a good ear, I'm a good listener." Alex stood to go back to his own bed. Then he turned to look back at Art, who had lain down on his back. "Art, would you tell me more about that girl you knew in high school? What was her name? Clarissa Mandez?"

Art rolled to one side and propped his chin up by resting

his hand. His arm leaned on one elbow. His coal-black eyes seemed darker than night as they glared into Alex's. Alex turned to walk back and climb under his own blankets.

Art's voice was hard as he spoke curtly. "Clarissa Mandez was like your goody old Maid Melissa Sanders, teacher's pet, Miss Special Privilege. She said that she was totally blind, but I don't think so. It was just an act to get attention. I even asked her out once, and she had the gall to turn me down. She claimed that she had to study. She got straight As practically. She had everyone eating out of her hand—except me!"

"Aren't you being a bit unfair, Art?"

"Unfair." Art snapped then pounced his fist into the mattress. "They were unfair to me—all of them—the teachers, the other kids, the social workers. I never got anything handed to me until they decided to work with my mother to plan for my college education. I am going to leave my mark, Alex. You wait and see."

"Take it easy, Art. I didn't mean to bring up bad memories."

"Then don't spark old flames. Let the memories lie. Besides, she is dead now anyway." Art slumped back onto his pillow.

"What? What do you mean, dead?" Alex sat up in his bed.

"Clarissa Mandez died in a fire at school during our senior year of high school. Now let the old ashes die, Alex. I have told you more than enough about my past. Good night, Alex."

"Good night, Art." Alex lay back too, but sleep eluded him for a long time. It seemed hours before his mind let him rest.

Looking back on the week between Christian fellowship meetings, Missy thought that the time had passed quickly. Contributing to her busy schedule was her newly acquired part-time job as a teacher's aide in the special education department of the Iandale Junior High School, five days a week. She had arranged for morning and late-afternoon classes to be free from noon to three o'clock for lunch and work. While she sat waiting for Alex to open the meeting, she reminded herself that she hadn't spent much time with him alone this semester.

The initial meeting had been a sharing time. Now, after his opening prayer and before the singing segment, Alex announced that the title of this gathering would be "All Things New." This was based on the fact that in Christ, we are a new creation.

Alex began his speech once the singing had concluded.

"Partaking of Christ's nature is a lifelong process, folks. From the moment that we trust God with our lives, by asking Christ to come into our hearts as Savior and Lord, He is at work in us, and He will be faithful to complete it until the day of Jesus Christ. That is, it will be a slow and continual process. God never gives up on us, so don't forget that He is the same yesterday, today, and forever. We are still human, still vulnerable, still changeable. He is not."

Alex paused and stood up to walk into the middle of the circle of chairs. He began to walk slowly around the inside of the circle, taking note of the relaxed faces of most of his brothers and sisters in their Christian commitment. The hard set of Art's jaw did not escape him as he continued to speak in his mild manner.

"What I'm trying to say, friends, is we can't base our commitment to Christ on emotion alone. Feelings and situations can change without prior planning. No one has to be reminded of the circumstances of last semester. We need an accurate knowledge of His Word to see us through, and we must apply it realistically and intelligently to our lives on a daily basis. The words of the Bible are real and pertinent for us today just as they were in the time of creation.

"Let's pray now and thank God for His steadfast and unchanging love for us as demonstrated by the free gift of eternal life in His Son Jesus Christ for all who believe."

"Wow!" Zoe had exclaimed to Missy after they had stood when the meeting was over. "I didn't think that God cares about me that much."

Missy nodded eagerly with a wide smile across her face.

"Hey, Zoe. You want to walk with me?" Art interrupted. "I want to talk with you. Alone."

"Sure, Art. I'm sure Missy and Alex won't mind."

"Well, come on then." Art held the door for Zoe to leave.

Missy and Alex, when left alone, began to fold chairs and stack them in the corner one by one. She looked forward to the routine of helping him after meetings now.

As they worked, she finally asked, "What's with Art? He left in a hurry."

"Hopefully, Zoe will be of more help to him than I was."

Missy heard the seriousness in Alex's tone. When he explained that Art had suddenly lost his mother during Christmas break and the fact that Art had no other close family, she then understood.

"Art needs to release his feelings. I hope he can with Zoe."

"We can pray for him." Missy grasped Alex's hands as he released the last chair to the stack.

When they finished praying, they were still holding hands.

"Alex, I know I haven't spent much time with you this term."

"I was wondering if you were avoiding being alone with me."

She shook her head.

"Missy, I want to ask you a personal question." He released her hands and folded his arms across his chest.

"Go ahead. You can ask me anything."

"Missy, are you still bothered by the attack on you last

semester? I mean, what about us?"

"Oh, no, that doesn't bother me now. I can handle it. Remember, I wasn't actually hurt—thanks to you and Todd—I was just scared. I didn't suffer the guilt and humiliation that a victim would. Mostly it is the teaching job for my special education class credit that is taking up extra time. Alex, I'm sorry. It has nothing to do with you, with us. Believe me, I have no intention of avoiding you. Alex? Well, I see that I'm just going to have to apologize properly." Missy tugged at his arms, but he had tightened his hold teasingly.

The inflection in his voice told her that he was smiling when he asked what she was trying to do.

"I'm trying to apologize, Alex. Now come down here where I can reach you."

She gave up on his arms and reached up to place her hands behind his head. At the warmth of her touch, he unfolded his arms to encircle her. Dipping his head, his lips met hers with a kiss that was neither teasing nor playful. Time ceased to exist for their moment of oneness. Then Alex drew in a shaky breath and moved to burrow his face into her thick hair. His wavy locks reminded her of golden silk as her fingers caressed them.

They stood holding each other silently. Time apart had, indeed, deepened their commitment to each other.

Finally, Missy whispered, "Alex, without you, a part of me is missing. I love you."

Alex pulled his head up to kiss her again. Then he said, "Oh, sweet Missy. When I hold you, it feels as if a weight has been lifted off my shoulders. You are right for me."

"Alex." She released her embrace to bring her hands up to touch his face. "Don't ever be afraid to talk to me, to tell me what you are feeling." She raised her mouth to his once more.

His arms were squeezing her, almost too tightly. "Oh,

Missy, I don't want to take you back to the girls' dorm. You know what I mean. I want us to be together always." Without waiting for her to respond, he released her abruptly and turned to go pick up their coats. The moisture in her eyes answered it for her when he returned with her red parka.

Missy was sitting up in bed reading when Zoe's blond head appeared above the top of her textbook. Missy removed her magnifying glass from the page and looked up. She could hear Zoe's deep voice, but the words blended together incoherently.

Missy climbed out of bed. "Wait a minute, Zo. I'll put one hearing aid back on so I can hear you clearly." Hurriedly she put down her book and glass to pick up the unit, place it behind her left ear, and stuff the mold into her ear. After turning it on, she said, "Okay, now, what did you say?"

Zoe had hung her coat in the closet and was undressing. She looked over at her roommate and smiled. "I am glad you are still up. Art was asking me some weird questions tonight. Did he tell you about his mother's death?"

Missy shook her head. "No. Alex did."

Zoe picked up her brush and sat on her own bed. "He must still be in shock or something. He wanted to know if I would forgive someone who had wronged me in some way. How should I know? I'd have to be in the situation to know what I'd do. I almost wonder if he was trying to ask if I would forgive my mother."

"Would you?"

"Huh? Would I what?"

"Would you forgive your mother for putting you up for adoption?"

Zoe stopped brushing her hair and looked at Missy. She began to shake her head slowly, although Missy didn't see it.

"I don't know." Zoe got up and clapped the brush down on

her bureau. "I hope she had a darn good reason for doing it. Besides, I'll probably never get the chance to find out what I'd do anyway."

Missy shrugged her shoulders and then asked, "What do you think Art was driving at?"

"Who knows." Zoe got into bed. "When I asked why he was asking such strange questions, he said he was testing reactions for a psych class report. His questions were awfully evasive though. I don't know what he expected. So how was your evening?"

Missy sighed and shook her head as a grin crept across her face. "Zoe, I don't know what to do. I think I'm falling in love with Alex."

"Gee, what a terrible fate. I wish I had such problems."

"You still don't understand, Zo. It takes me twice as long to do my studying as the average student. I'm trying to get started in a career, and now with a job, too, I can't afford to spend a lot of time with Alex. Yet I want to more and more."

"Well then, why don't you ask him to study with you?"

"I don't know if that would work. I mean, would we spend more time talking or studying? Besides, I hadn't even thought of asking him since I turned him down last semester." She got up to replace her hearing aid on the bureau and turn off her bed lamp. "Maybe I will," Missy said half to herself as she got back into bed. "Good night, Zo."

"Night, Missy."

As she snuggled under her blankets, Missy decided to call Alex first thing the next morning.

In her sleep state, Missy heard voices calling to her, whispering her name. She tried to open her eyes but could not. Turning on her right side facing the wall, she buried her head deeper into the pillow, trying to dismiss the voices.

Then she found herself standing in the middle of a dirt track with grassy fields running alongside in vast expanse and woods beyond. Alex's voice startled her from behind.

"It's over, Melissa."

She turned to face him, sensing his anger from his sharp tone.

"What do you mean, Alex? I don't understand."

"Don't play innocent with me. You know what I'm talking about. It's over between us. Art was right, you little egotist. You're just like all the other girls. And I thought you were different." He turned and started to walk away. At her protests, Alex turned back only long enough to add, "Ha, it won't work this time. I see through you now. Find your own way back. You're on your own now. Goodbye, old maid."

"No, Alex, wait. Please wait." He walked on.

As fear and desolation gripped her, Missy found herself standing in front of the mirror above her and Zoe's adjoining set of bureau drawers in their room at Falcon Hall. She blinked her eyes. What was that brown blob behind her reflection? She turned to see a tall uniformed, faceless figure standing at the foot of her bed. Missy tried to scream, but no sound escaped.

While she stared, the arm raised a hand holding... a clock? Yes, it was a clock. She could see its bleak face, black with white numbers. The hands, pointing to 1:50— it had to be a.m.—seemed to be mocking her with a smile. The figure was fiddling with the back of the clock with its other hand. Then, as the insistent ticking grew louder, the clock was suddenly hurled toward her. Surprising herself, Missy caught it. With sudden dread, Missy realized that it wasn't just an ordinary clock but a time bomb! As the explosion began to rumble in her head, she uttered a cry of panic that finally woke her from the nightmare.

Sitting upright in bed, Missy blinked, touched her chest,

and scratched herself to be sure that she was really awake. Her heart was still racing. The dryness in her throat and the throbbing ache in her head convinced Missy to get up and go to the bathroom for water. The cool linoleum under her feet assured her of reality as she slipped on her yellow robe. As her feet padded softly along the dimly lit hallway on dark-green carpeting, Missy glanced repeatedly over her shoulder.

What would you do if you had no one to turn to? The thought persisted. *Nowhere to turn for help if you desperately needed it? No family, like Zoe, no friends, no job?*

Upon entering the bathroom, she went to one of the sinks and turned on the cold-water faucet. The water began to pour out in a thunderous rush, and she turned the faucet to slow its fall. An overwhelming urge to cry welled up inside when Missy recalled her despairing conversation with Alex in her recent dream. She fought it and lost. Splashing water on her face finally calmed her enough to take her aspirin. How could she have allowed herself to feel so deeply for one man? After she turned off the water, she whirled around half-expecting to encounter the tall uniformed figure. Shaking her head, she told herself not to be foolish and left the bathroom. The phrase "Nowhere to turn" echoed in her thoughts while the lurking aloneness of the wee morning hour surrounded her.

After closing the door to her room very softly, Missy felt along the desks until she came to her chair and sat down. She clicked on her desk light. The unique design of the rooms in this dorm allowed one person to study and not wake the other. Opening her notebook, she took a pen and wrote down the haunting phrase, "Nowhere to Turn." Writing would occupy her mind. She sighed softly and then began to think and then to write. After about half an hour, she was well on her way to writing a poem, or maybe it would be a skit.

Satisfied with her progress, Missy went back to bed with something to occupy her mind. Zoe was still sleeping, she was sure.

With the memory of her nightmare still feeding her headache, Missy walked slowly down the stairs to the lobby the next morning. If Alex and Todd hadn't rescued her from that attack last semester, she surely would have had nowhere to turn for help.

Only Jesus, she reminded herself.

Did she love Alex that deeply, she wondered, or was she mistaking gratitude for love?

When she reached for the outside door handle, Missy remembered that she had intended to call Alex first. Releasing the cold handle, she turned to walk past the desk with the mailboxes behind it and go to the pay phone that stood in the back corner next to the maintenance office. Stopping in front of the wall phone, she felt inside her shoulder bag for her change purse. Finding it, she took out some quarters then replaced the purse in its pouch and closed the bag. She shifted the weight of her books and portable tape recorder, which aided in note-taking, and felt for the coin slot with her left hand. As she manipulated a coin with her fingers, it slipped from her grasp and clinked to the floor, but she did not hear the sound. In fact, she heard no sound at all. It was after 6:15 a.m., and yet no one was out and about except her, it seemed. Students were not yet rushing downstairs to venture out into the cold January air.

"Oh, great." Missy stooped to set down her belongings and feel around the floor for her lost quarter. When her fingers ran along the hard smoothness of the tiles, they slid on a slippery surface.

She withdrew her hand quickly, startled by the unexpected texture. Peering closely at the blue-and-white tiles beneath her knees, she still could not see what she had touched.

Again Missy reached out to search with her hand. This time she ventured to pick up the slippery thing. Holding it closely in front of her face, she recognized it as a small square of deep-yellow cellophane.

"Hmp. Just a candy wrapper." Again her fingers felt around.

Missy gasped involuntarily as she became increasingly aware of slow, deliberate footsteps approaching from behind her. Her heart began to pound. Still shaken by her dream, she began to wonder irrationally if the man who had plagued the campus last semester had escaped and returned to cause more harm. While still on her knees, Missy turned slowly to face—she was sure—her attacker.

12

Be My Valentine

Missy could feel the color fading from her cheeks as her gaze went from light-brown boots and traveled up long-legged blue jeans. Her heart pounded harder as she stood up slowly. She thought fleetingly that she was grateful that she had put on a pantsuit this morning in anticipation of the cold weather. Now she remembered how easily her attacker of less than a month ago had tossed up her skirt and torn into her defenseless nylons. Her mind stopped rambling with a shock of recognition when her eyes met a bright-blue parka and above it a smiling face topped with sunny-blond hair.

"Alex?" Her tone indicated disbelief.

"I wondered how long it would take you to recognize me. I came by early, hoping to catch you before you went to breakfast. Hey, are you okay?"

"I . . . I . . . thought that you were some stranger coming to attack me. I'm sorry." Now her cheeks had too much color. "Don't mind me. I'm okay."

"Oh, Missy, I'm sorry. I didn't realize. Next time I'll tell you who I am."

"I guess I'm being a little foolish, Alex. I wouldn't be so jumpy except for the nightmare I had last night." Then she smiled at him. "Oh, could you please find the coin I dropped on the floor? So far I've only been able to find a butterscotch candy wrapper that startled me. I mean, I didn't expect to touch something of that nature looking for a coin. Then I heard footsteps, and you came along to scare me half to death."

"Oh, you want me to save the other half for later?" he teased.

When he spied the quarter, he stooped to pick it up. Also he gathered up her books and tape recorder to hand to her. They both turned when they heard a door open nearby and saw Joe Burns step out into their corner section of the lobby from the maintenance office.

When he saw them, he teased, "Now, now, no neckin' in the corner, you two."

Missy smiled. The sound of his gruff voice pleased her. Instantly, she thought of Ashley. "How are you doing, Joe? It is good to see you. I hardly ever see you around campus these days."

"That's because you're too busy runnin' off somewhere. I see you, though," Joe retorted.

"I don't doubt it," Missy replied.

"Joe, how's the construction, or should I say, reconstruction, coming on your house?"

"Not fast enough for me, Alex. Not that the Babettes haven't been wonderful to Ashley and me. I just miss the old place. Lots of memories. Anyway, it looks like another couple of months' wait. I think those guys should work on one job at a time and not work on so many."

"Well, I'm sure you can stay at the Babettes' as long as you need to. We will be out to visit you again. See you later, Joe."

Joe nodded goodbye as Alex and Missy headed out into the frigid January day.

"Where's your roommate this morning?" Alex asked as they walked.

"Oh, Zoe doesn't have a class until later this morning, so I didn't want to wake her. We are out earlier than usual, you know, Alex. We will probably have at least a twenty-minute wait until the dining commons open at seven o'clock."

"I wanted to make time to see you since you are so busy during the day."

"Busy. That is becoming an understatement. This is one of my busiest days three times a week with four classes and teaching. Alex, I wanted to ask you about Art. Do you think he'll be okay? I think his mother's death hit pretty hard. Zoe said he was asking some strange questions the other night."

Alex nodded then answered. "Yeah, I'm kinda worried about him too. He isn't letting anyone get close to his feelings. He needs to open up to somebody for his own good. I hope he'll confide in Zoe."

"Speaking of Zoe, when I had the opportunity, I brought up her feelings toward her mother."

"Now, Melissa, don't push too fast. Let Dr. Francis handle it in her own way." Upon reaching the dining commons, Alex tried to open the double doors, but they were still locked.

"We must be crazy to be out this early." Missy chattered her teeth for emphasis.

"Yeah, crazy in love."

She returned his warming smile. "Alex, I do love you, more than I realized. That's why I was so upset this morning." Her expression had turned serious. She paid no attention to the line of students that was forming behind them. "In my dream you were angry enough to break up with me. Then some faceless thing threw a bomb at me, and I woke up. I didn't want to go back to sleep after that, so I started to do some writing."

"For Dr. Francis's class?" Alex prompted.

She shook her head. "No, just for me, a poem or sketch."

Alex tried the double doors again, but they were still locked. "May I meet you here for lunch, Missy? I only have a couple of classes this morning. Besides, it will be warmer outside by then."

"Very funny," she retorted. "Okay, but don't sneak up on me."

"I won't, fair lady. I promise." In mock chivalry, he bowed deeply.

As he bent forward, one of his books slid to the ground. At that moment, someone from inside the building opened the dining room doors, almost knocking Alex off balance. Missy gripped his arm to aid his quick recovery as they both stumbled inside ahead of an impatient line of hungry students.

"Alex, you okay?"

"Oh, sure." His tone was sharp. "I just made a complete fool of myself. I'm just great."

"No, honey, it didn't look that bad. No one was watching. Really." Missy's attempt to ease his embarrassment was clearly not successful. "I do things like that all the time. You get used to it."

"Forget it." His tone was still sharp. He stepped to the serving area, pulled a tray from the rack as he passed, and read the breakfast menu as he moved.

The days were passing quickly. Preparations as leader of the Christian fellowship group took up much of Alex's spare time. Desiring to help his roommate through this time of personal loss, Alex began to pay closer attention to Art's behavior. He tried to be discreet enough so that Art wouldn't suspect him. Alex wondered why Art spent so much time doing research at the Iandale Public Library instead of using the one on campus, but he didn't question his roommate about it. Art was very much in Alex's personal prayers as was Missy.

Missy and Zoe both had full schedules of their own. Missy was enthusiastic and grateful that Zoe was willing and eager to have a regular Bible study with her several evenings a week. Missy believed strongly that regular study was important to build a firm foundation of faith. She remained inspired by her nurturing from Laurie during the previous school year. In spite of her busy schedule, Missy still found time to write and perfect her piece titled "Nowhere to Turn." She had decided to submit it to the Junior High School committee for their annual play.

One afternoon in early February, Zoe returned to the room to find Missy sitting at her desk with chin in hands, staring at her bulletin board. Zoe plumped her own books down on her desk and slid out of her coat.

Looking at Missy, she asked, "What's the matter with you?"

"I've been rejected." Missy continued to stare. "My piece wasn't good enough for the Junior High's committee."

"Hey, that's just one opinion. Besides, what do they know about good literature anyway? Oh, here." Zoe handed her a plain white envelope with her name typed on it. "You should check your mailbox more often, Missy."

"Thanks."

Missy took her magnifying glass from her purse to look at the typed envelope, which said simply, "Melissa Sanders."

"Looks like it was hand-delivered."

She ripped it open and took her magnifier to read the typed verse.

"Well, it is certainly appropriate. It says that there is a time to live and a time to die. I bombed out with my skit at school. This is a reminder from Ecclesiastes chapter 3. I wonder who sent this note. It isn't signed." She opened the bottom desk drawer and tossed the note along with the envelope and her cassette from class into it. Then she closed the draw again. "Any more good news?"

"That's a weird note to send to somebody," Zoe said. Then she added thoughtfully, "Why don't you show your play to Dr. Francis? Maybe you can at least get some extra credit."

Missy looked up. "You really think I should?"

"Sure." Zoe stood up. "I'm going to change for supper. Alex is meeting you here, right?"

Missy nodded. "Is it that late already? Jeans will be warmer than a dress." She got up to change also. "I'm sorry, Zo. I guess I was feeling sorry for myself."

"We all do it," Zoe confessed. "Just don't make a habit of it." Zoe smiled. "Gee, Missy. I wish I could get my locket back. I've been praying about it, you know."

Missy began pulling her brush through the long strands of dark-brown hair. "Only God knows His timing, Zo. We just have to pray and trust His judgment."

A few minutes later, a loud knock broke the silence.

A look at Zoe told Missy that her roommate was ready too, and she hurried around to open the door at the other end of the room. With a quick hi, she reached up to greet Alex with a memorable hug. Her cheeks colored when she noticed a tall black-haired man in a gray parka standing in the hallway away from the open door. She was sure that his coal-black eyes were scrutinizing her.

"Oh. Hi, Art." She drew back.

"Is Zoe here?" Art asked, ignoring her greeting. "Alex talked me into going to supper with you people for a change."

"That's great." Missy smiled.

"Yeah, I'm ready. Good to see you, Art." Zoe stepped out into the hallway and slipped her hand inside Art's arm. They headed for the stairs while Missy closed and locked the door.

Alex gave her a quick kiss. "Don't let him bug you, honey."

She smiled up at him and tucked her hand under his arm. "Alex, I wanted to tell you that the school committee rejected my skit for their play. I was disappointed, but..."

"Maybe the Lord has something better for it," he interjected.

She squeezed his arm as they started to walk toward the stairs after Art and Zoe.

Art had wanted a secluded spot if possible, so Alex found a corner table in a back row that wasn't occupied. This section of the dining room was not crowded when they sat down.

"I was surprised to see butterscotch brownies for dessert," Missy commented while dunking her tea bag.

"Yeah, but pork chops again," Zoe complained.

Art said nothing but proceeded to strip bare his baked potato with fork and knife.

"I have an idea," Alex announced. "Why don't we put on a play ourselves this spring here on campus?"

The others turned surprised expressions on him.

He continued to elaborate, "Missy's skit could be a group activity performed by our Christian fellowship group. What do you think?"

"Alex," Missy protested, "you haven't even read it yet. How do you know if you will want to use it?"

"Well, isn't it a Christian play?" He picked up his pork chop to bite into it.

Missy nodded before sipping her tea. After carefully replacing her cup, she shrugged her shoulders as if apprehensive of the idea.

"So what's it about?" Art finally joined the conversation.

Both surprised and encouraged by his question, Missy began to explain. "Well, it came about as a result of a bad dream. The idea is, what would you do if everyone turned away from you—your family, friends, boss, even spouse—you would have nowhere to turn unless you were a Christian relying on Jesus."

She did not see Alex's intent gaze watching her enthusiasm grow as she spoke. Knowingly, Zoe smiled.

"Hmm. Not a bad point," Art admitted.

"I could make a couple of copies if you and Alex would like to read it," Missy offered. She held her fork in midair, as if daring her piece of potato to fall should Art give the wrong answer.

"It's up to Alex. I don't care," Art said.

Missy still held her fork.

"Of course we want to read it," Alex replied.

"Sounds good," Zoe agreed. "I already read it."

Missy finished her potato. Seeing Alex get up, she asked, "Alex, would you bring back a couple more brownies? I assume you're going back for seconds?" Then she smiled.

"Some for me too?" Zoe smiled sweetly.

Alex grinned. "Art, you want something?"

"Whatdya think? You know I like butterscotch, Alex."

All smiles prevailed when Alex returned with an extra plate of brownies along with a second helping of the main course for himself. He set the dessert plate in the middle of the table.

"How did you manage to sneak off with all these?" Zoe asked.

"Oh, I just grabbed a few." He resumed his seat across from Missy.

"Alex," Missy asked, "do you really think the group will go along with acting out my skit in front of an audience?"

"It doesn't hurt to try, honey. After I read it, I'll bring it up at the next meeting."

"Mmm." Zoe nodded while chewing her brownie. After finishing, she added, "Missy is going to talk to Dr. Francis about it too."

"Vying for extra credit in creative writing class, no doubt."

Missy shook her head. "No, Art. I want a professional opinion of my work."

"Who knows. I might be dating a future famous playwright," Alex said.

Missy laughed.

"You had better be careful, Alex. She could turn out to be the wolf in sheep's clothing." Art paused deliberately and then cleared his throat. Then he added, "Come to steal, kill, and devour all the brownies."

Missy said nothing, trying not to reveal the sting of the knife that had just been thrust into her heart. She was not aware of Alex's intense gaze upon her. He could see the pain in her eyes.

Zoe's voice intruded on her thoughts, saying, "I don't get it."

"Read John chapter 10," Missy said flatly. "It's a twisted version of verse 10."

Alex replaced his teacup on the tray and rested his hand on the table beside it. He was still looking at Missy when he spoke. "That's funny, I thought she was an angel whom God Himself has chosen just for me."

That endearing blush colored her cheeks. It contrasted well with her broadening smile, he thought. Her right hand reached across the table to close around his left.

"Thanks, Alex, but you know very well that I can't be an angel. Angels and humans are two completely different orders of created beings."

"Missy, didn't you tell me something about the Bible being our sword?" Zoe asked innocently.

"Ephesians chapter 6," the other three chimed in unison.

"So what are you doing after supper, Missy?" Alex asked. They were still holding hands.

She shrugged her shoulders.

"Let's all do something different," Zoe suggested.

"Such as?" Art inquired in his deep, nasal-sounding voice.

"Why don't we go swimming?" Zoe continued, "There is open swim at the gym tonight from seven to nine o'clock. I saw it posted on the bulletin board."

"What? Swimming in Feb—burr—ary?" Missy exaggerated. She looked at Alex.

"I guess we could." His tone was thoughtful. He released Missy's hand and turned to Art and then Zoe who had made the suggestion.

"Suppose so," Art said.

"I'm game. I mean, I'll go," Zoe assured the others.

"Okay then, let's get going," Missy decided. She loved to swim.

They rose to leave the dining commons.

Later that week, Missy sat in her creative writing teacher's office for the appointment she had set to discuss her skit.

"Thank you for taking the extra time for this, Barbara."

"Oh, you are very welcome." Dr. Francis put the paper back down on the desk and looked up to smile at Missy. "I am always glad to see extra initiative from a student. Missy, this is good quality work. I would say it has definite potential."

"Really?" Missy exclaimed excitedly.

Dr. Francis nodded slowly with exaggerated motion for Missy to see it. "What reason did the school committee give you for not accepting it?"

"They said it wouldn't suit their needs."

"Do you know why, Missy?"

"No."

"What is your emphasis, Missy? Think."

"The point is that you always have Jesus to turn to even when you think you have no one and nothing left. You can turn to Him no matter what."

Dr. Francis smiled at Missy's enthusiasm. "Then it has a Christian emphasis, right?"

"Of course." The statement was so matter-of-fact. Missy said to herself, *I wouldn't write anything else.*

"Missy, it wasn't the quality of your work that got you a rejection. It was your emphasis. Public schools shy away from using Christian or religious material."

Dr. Francis smiled at the surprised look on her student's face.

"I didn't even think of that. Thank you, Dr. Francis, Barbara. You know, I gave Alex a copy of it to read. He suggested that the Christian fellowship group act it out as a spring benefit."

"Now you are targeting the right market. Oh, by the way, I wanted to tell you that Todd is going to lecture in the science building some night soon. I'll let you know when he has arranged it in his business schedule."

"Great. I'll be sure to go." Missy stood.

"Missy, there is one more thing." Dr. Francis leaned forward in her chair. It groaned at her effort. "I want to have a talk with Zoe as soon as I can get my courage up. I would like you to be present when I do. All right?"

"Yes, I understand, Barbara. I'll be praying about it."

"Thank you, Missy. Here. Don't forget to take your skit." She smiled warmly as she handed the papers to the younger woman.

When the office door had closed behind Missy, Dr. Francis

sighed and propped her elbows up on top of her desk. She folded her hands in front of her face.

"Lord, I envy her. I wish that I had her enthusiasm and assurance of faith."

Sleep could be a fickle, elusive creature. Alex rolled onto his back and stretched his arms up under his pillow. His bedcovers whispered soft solitude when he sat up. He could hear his roommate lightly snoring in the bed across from him. From his nightstand draw, Alex took out a book light and his copy of Missy's play "Nowhere to Turn." From the first stanza, his emotions were caught, cast down, and then uplifted by the implication. The opening screamed in utter desolation only to be resurrected by the chorus. The second stanza plunged into deep hurt and despair. Then the repeated hope of the chorus rang out.

The words blurred, and Alex set the papers down on the bed momentarily to wipe his eyes. He took a deep breath and picked up the play to resume reading.

The third stanza spoke of success followed by emptiness and then the repeated chorus. The fourth and final stanza reminded readers of the finality of death without the blessed hope in Jesus's resurrection. Alex reread the repeated refrain to himself:

Only Jesus, only Jesus can turn your life around.
Take mixed emotions and reverse the upside down feelings.
Take the fire from the pain.
Only Jesus.

When he had finished reading, Alex replaced the light and copy in his drawer and settled back down under his blankets.

"Lord," he breathed quietly, "I know it's right." He hugged his pillow, waiting for the subtle approach of sleep.

"Hey, Missy. Wait a minute."

Missy was hurrying toward the lobby door to exit Falcon Hall. Hearing a voice, she stopped and turned to look around.

"It's Sue, Laurie's roommate. I have desk duty today."

"Oh." Missy walked back toward the desk. "What's up?"

"Don't forget to check your mailbox today," Sue replied. "You might find something. It's Valentine's Day, you know."

Missy waved a hand. "Maybe later. I don't have time now. I don't want to be late for school."

"I'll still be here later. Don't forget." Sue called after her.

Upon her return that afternoon, Missy walked into the lobby to find Zoe, Laurie, and several other girls all standing around talking and giggling. Susan was still behind the desk.

"What's this?" Missy asked. Sitting on top of the desk was a large open heart-shaped box filled with butterscotch candies all individually wrapped in deep-yellow cellophane.

Zoe stepped closer to her roommate. "It's for all of us in the dorm. Here read the card." Zoe took the accompanying card from under the box and handed it to Missy.

Missy whipped out her magnifier to examine it.

On the front was a burning heart cartoon picture. Above it the printed words read, "I'm on fire over you, Valentine." Opening it, she read inside in red ink, "Happy Valentine's Day, girls, from your friendly fire marshal, Arthur Wills."

"Help yourself," Sue offered. Then she asked, "Are you ready to check your own mailbox now? You must have gotten something from Alex."

Missy also smiled. "All right, but I'm not expecting

anything."

"Sure. Sure," Zoe teased. She walked behind Susan to check her own box. "Oh my goodness!" she exclaimed excitedly. "I got something." She brought a small square box wrapped in red tissue paper around front to open it.

Missy found a note in her box to pick up packages from the desk clerk. Sue obliged by handing her two large boxes. One was heart-shaped and wrapped in yellow tissue paper, Missy's favorite color. The other was a long, rectangle shape and was wrapped in red tissue.

"Are you sure these are both mine, Sue?" She began to remove the envelopes to read the cards first.

"Hurry up," Laurie urged. "I already opened mine. Pete Early sent me a sweet card and candy. I was surprised to receive that."

"You first, Zoe," Missy said as she read her cards.

Zoe tore into the paper. Her eyes widened as she opened the little box. After examining it carefully, Zoe slipped her long-lost beehive necklace around her neck. The plastic queen bee was still intact.

Looking up, she said, "I almost can't believe it. I have had a prayer answered. I got my necklace back!"

Burying her face momentarily behind the open paper, she read the enclosed note to herself. It explained that Art had found the necklace outside on the ground and was returning it to her.

Missy had read the card accompanying the long, rectangular box. On the front was pictured an alarm clock in the shape of a heart with the words captioned above it, "Time is running out." On the inside, it read, "To be my Valentine." Under the printing was typed, "For Clarissa Sanders."

It was unsigned. Missy said nothing while she tore into the paper to open the long box. Inside lay a long-stemmed rose that was charred black and had broken petals. Missy made a face and replaced the box cover. She passed a hand over her eyes.

"Who would play such a mean prank?" Zoe asked.

"Don't know." Missy shook her head. "It was unsigned. I . . . I'll just put the card with my other note. She stuffed the card and envelope into her purse without letting anyone else see it."

"The nerve of some people," Laurie observed. "The jerk didn't even have the courage to sign it."

"Please, don't say anything to Alex, any of you," Missy pleaded. "It isn't worth the hurt. Just forget it."

Missy smiled when she read the other card. The front said simply, "Be My Valentine." It pictured a boy and girl in silhouette kissing. On the inside, she read, "For the sweetest heart I know. From Alexander with love." Missy gasped when she opened the box to find her favorite milk chocolate mint candies.

"That's more like it," Laurie said.

Applause and cheers met Alex, Art, and Pete as they entered the lobby a few minutes later.

Zoe went up to Art and took his hands. "Thank you, Art. I never thought I'd see this again."

He returned her smile.

"Gosh, Pete, I don't know what to say." Laurie had stepped close to give him a quick, casual kiss on the cheek. Then she stepped back.

"Now, wait a minute, Laurie. Would you like to go for a walk and practice that thank-you a little more?" Pete grinned innocently.

Giggles ensued.

Missy walked up to Alex and put her arms around his neck. "Thank you, Alexander, and I've had a lot of practice." She met his eager lips with loving caresses.

Pete cleared his throat. "So anyway, Laurie, Missy, and Zoe, your Prince Charming have come to take you out to dinner tonight at the diner. My carriage awaits." He made a sweeping gesture with his hand.

    Surprised and pleased, the girls went upstairs to deposit their gifts—with the exception of one anonymously received by Missy—and to change to go out with their beaux.

13

A Spark of Reality

Alex smiled at the bewildered look that Missy was giving him. Following their companionable meal at the diner, Pete had dropped them off in front of the Iandale common as Alex had previously arranged with Pete.

"Alex, it's only about eighteen degrees out here according to the radio. Isn't it a little strange to be walking in the park at nine thirty at night in February?" Missy asked him.

"I figured we could use the exercise."

They walked arm in arm, silently, slowly for a time.

Finally, Missy commented, "I don't like to be cold, but I love the snow. I like to listen to the crunch when I walk on it."

"Are you cold?" Alex stopped walking and came to stand in front of her.

She shook her head and smiled up into his face.

"Missy, there is something I want to ask you."

"Oh, oh. What is it?" Impulsively, she stood on tiptoe to give him a light kiss.

In response, his lips pressed against hers again and his

arms enfolded her snugly. Murmuring softly into her hair, Alex hugged her tightly. Then he proposed. "Missy, I love you, and I want you to be my wife. Will you marry me?"

He felt her body tremble and her arms tighten around him. "Hey, don't cry," he said. "You'll form icicles."

When she had quieted, she brought her hands up to rub her eyes with her mittens. "I love you so much, Alex. I just can't believe you really . . . Oh, yes, darling, forever and ever." Then, remembering several previous conversations, she asked, "Alex, wasn't there something else you wanted to tell me, something important?"

"No, nothing, sweetheart." His arms hugged her closer to him.

Alex had deluded himself into thinking that it didn't really matter. He might never have to tell her what his immediate family, his physician, and only a few others knew.

Art had gone upstairs with Zoe, saying he had something to discuss with her in private. That left Pete and Laurie in the lobby with the desk clerk on duty.

"So, Laurie, would you mind waiting here with me for a while?" Pete asked her. "I told Alex I'd wait for him here to go back to our dorm."

"Sure, Pete. Thanks for tonight. I'll never forget it."

They walked over to a couch that was located behind the staircase to sit down.

Encouraged by her smile, Pete asked, "Laurie, would you go out with me again, maybe just the two of us this time?"

She nodded and leaned back against the cushion. "It's nice to have a break from studying and working at the bookstore. You don't seem to have a lot of free time either, Pete. Seems you're always working on a story."

His grin spread his freckles, making them more noticeable.

"I haven't had much reason for free time before now."

Laurie shrugged her shoulders. "Well, let's compare class schedules," she suggested.

"I could pick you up here to go to the Christian fellowship group meetings," Pete offered.

"Now, that's not very practical," Laurie replied. "You want to walk all the way over here to Falcon Hall when the meetings are being held in your own dorm?" His eyes met and held hers with a compelling look. In a softer tone, she suggested, "Pete, if you are going to walk all the way over here, why don't we just go to supper together that night?"

"Great idea. I'll hold you to that arrangement." He smiled for a moment then began to speak again. "Laurie, I . . ." he hesitated.

"Yes, Pete?" She was studying his face as if she had just now recognized him for the first time.

"Nothing. We have time to get acquainted, I mean. I don't graduate until June."

Other couples entered the lobby to part company or meet to leave together, but Peter Early was unaware. Usually, Early Bird Pete observed everything around him, mentally noting details and storing information, but not now. Now he had only one person on his usually inquisitive mind. Pete looked up when Laurie's hand slapped his knee.

"Pay attention, Peter. Zoe is talking to you."

"Oh, I'm sorry. What did you say, Zoe?" He hadn't noticed that Zoe and Art had come back downstairs.

"I wanted to know if you are going to wait for Alex and Missy to come back. They are crazy to be out in this cold."

"Ya. Alex doesn't think too clearly where Melissa is concerned, I'm afraid," Art observed.

"Can't say that I'd blame him," Pete said and then smiled

agreeably. "I don't think he'd like it if we left him here to walk back alone, Art, after I agreed to wait for him. It's different being with your girl."

"Ya, sure." Art made a face, and the girls laughed.

Zoe recognized the two approaching figures as she glanced out of the large window in front of her.

"Here they come now," she announced. "They're stuck together like two bees on honey."

Alex opened the metal door and followed Missy inside. He gestured toward the small group.

"Hey, I'm glad you are all here. We have something to tell you."

Pete rose. Clearing his throat for emphasis, he asked, "Is this an official statement, Mr. Marcus?"

"I'll wait for you guys in the car," Art said quickly. Without waiting for a response, he brushed past Alex and left the building.

"What's the matter with him?" Laurie asked.

"Ah, he's probably just edgy," Zoe replied. Then she turned toward Alex. "Are you meeting Missy here in the morning?"

He nodded briefly.

"Good. I want to talk to you."

He agreed.

"Well, what is this news?" Pete prompted.

Alex smiled and then announced proudly, "Missy and I are engaged to be married!"

Missy and Laurie hugged each other amid tears of joy.

Alex folded his arms across his chest and shook his head.

The others smiled patiently.

"When?" Zoe finally asked.

Missy turned to her roommate. "That's a good question." The implication of her decision began to take hold.

Alex chuckled quietly. "The sooner, the better."

"But we should wait until we finish school," Missy said.

"What? You mean, this summer?" Alex asked.

"No, Alex, I mean, graduate. *Finish* school." She emphasized the word *finish*.

Seeing Alex's shattered look, Pete spoke. "Now, now, you two, you have plenty of time to decide. Take it easy. You know, one step at a time."

"Yeah, that's true," Alex agreed. "So I'll meet you girls here tomorrow morning. How about quarter of seven?"

"That's fine." Missy stepped close to him for a final good night kiss.

Zoe waved and started upstairs smiling.

"Well, good night, Pete." Laurie's eyes were laughing as she held out her hand teasingly for him to shake it.

Pete was smiling as he shook his head. "Oh, no, not that way." He stepped closer to her and slipped his arms easily around her waist. They stood close to the same height as their lips came together, gently at first, then deeper.

After watching the girls depart, Alex and Pete went outside to the stinging reality of the cold evening air. They found Art leaning back against the back seat upholstery, so Alex got into the front passenger seat with Pete driving. Art stirred from his solitary thoughts when Pete started the engine.

"Well, Art, Missy and I are engaged to be married," Alex told his roommate.

"Alex, you didn't. You idiot! I told you. She is not what she seems to be."

Alex turned a glaring stare on his roommate while Pete drove. "Come on, Art. You're not going to start that discrimination stuff again, are you?"

"Fine." Art's impatience flared. "Don't listen to me. You'll be sorry you took up with her."

"Arthur Wills, I'm surprised at you," Pete interrupted their verbal duel. "People who have disabilities have the same rights as we do."

"And more privileges," Art snapped.

"The frustrations outweigh the privileges," Alex commented.

Pete blinked and kept his eyes on the road ahead. He hoped his face did not betray his surprise at Alex's perceptive statement.

"How would you know, Alex?" Art countered.

"Wouldn't you be surprised. The problems faced by people with disabilities—whether they are cognitive, physical, sensory, mental, or emotional—are just as real to them as anyone else's problems, no matter how slight or severe they might seem to ignorant bystanders."

"Alex, how did you become so perceptive on disabilities?" Pete asked.

"Never mind, Pete," Alex snapped irritably. Then he turned his head toward the back seat. "Besides, Art, you haven't even taken the time to get to know Missy."

"I don't have to. They're all alike."

"Now, Art," Pete tried to keep his tone light, "beware of the stereotype."

"You know, Art, you should think about changing your major. Your psychology stinks." Alex turned back to stare out of the passenger side window in the front where he was sitting.

The next morning, Alex was already waiting for the girls in the lobby even though they were five minutes early coming downstairs.

"Sleep well?" he asked while cuddling Missy in his arms.

"Mmm. I did, but Zoe had that nightmare about the haunted

house again."

Looking at Zoe, Alex could see the redness in her eyes and the strained muscle tension in her face.

"It's gotta be that necklace," Zoe insisted. "I took it off this morning and put it in my purse."

"I tried to tell her not to believe in superstition," Missy said as she released her embrace.

"Alex, I have to talk to you about Art," Zoe pleaded.

"Go on," Alex encouraged her.

"Let's go over here out of the way." Zoe led the way toward the corner of the lobby where the pay phone stood next to the maintenance office. Lowering her voice, Zoe explained, "Art told me that he was the one who had taken my necklace. I thought Christians didn't do things like that."

"Why would he want to steal your necklace?" Missy asked.

Alex chose to answer Zoe's question first. "Being Christian doesn't make us immune to sin, Zoe. Don't forget that in every situation, we still have freedom of choice. God doesn't force us to do anything. We obey or disobey by free will. Did Art say why he took your necklace?"

Zoe was watching his face intently. Art's confession had stunned her, but Alex was taking it in stride.

"Yeah, first he said he had taken it because he wanted to analyze it because it was so unusual and unique. Then, on impulse, he had given it to his mother for a Christmas gift. After she died, he felt that he should return it, but he wasn't sure how he was going to tell me."

"How did he get it in the first place? You wore it almost all the time, Zo," Missy said.

"He said that he took it on impulse one time while he was searching the rooms for bombs during one of the false alarms last semester. I had left it on top of the bureau several times when I went to take a shower and didn't put it back on usually until the next morning. Of course, when the alarm went off, I forgot about it."

"You're lucky you got it back, and with an explanation too."

"I know, Alex."

"Zoe, what did you tell Art after he confessed?"

Zoe smiled at Missy. "I know. You want to know if I forgave him, right? I did."

"Good."

"Being a Christian is a continual growth process," Alex said. "Now, how about breakfast?"

Since Alex wasn't carrying any books, both girls took an arm, and they proceeded to start the day.

Time passed like clockwork. Weeks ticked by. Finally, winter's chilling grip yielded to the sloshy touch of spring.

It was a tranquil Saturday afternoon when Alex and Missy walked out to the Iandale County fairgrounds. The muddy path beckoned their feet to remain, linger awhile longer, as it drew each step deeper into uncertainty.

"It won't be long now until I get . . . I mean, bring my bike back to school. You said you know how to ride, right, Missy?"

Missy smiled and nodded. She remembered herself as a scrawny six-year-old complaining that she would never learn to balance on two wheels. She also remembered her grandfather, with the patience of a fisherman, encouraging her to try again.

"My grandfather taught me."

Alex shook his head. "It took me a long time to learn balance. My dad and mom were encouragers, though. My mom died when I was sixteen. My brother Ben was twelve at the time. You remind me of my mom. Maybe that's why I was attracted to you so easily."

She stopped walking to stand close to him. "Alexander Marcus, you have my heart. Now, please don't break it."

With a passionate groan, he pulled her against him. The quick impulse was so forceful that it almost took her breath away.

"Oh, Missy. Sometimes I get the feeling that something dreadful is going to pull us apart. Just hold me for a while." He yielded his face to the security of her shoulder.

They stood for a long time locked in close embrace as if they were trying to steal from the relentless ticking of time. Finally, Alex straightened and loosened his hold somewhat.

"I'm sorry, honey. I don't know what comes over me. Sometimes I get these overwhelming feelings. I guess I'm insecure."

"Alex, listen to me," Missy spoke clearly and distinctly. "I love you no matter what. Honestly."

Their lips sealed again their promise of commitment.

For a time, they walked in silence, each with his and her own thoughts, savoring togetherness. Finally, Alex broke the silence.

"By the way, I read the notice in Parker Hall yesterday about the lecture Todd Francis is giving on fire safety. It will be next Friday night in the science building auditorium."

Missy laughed and then said, "Well, better late than not at all, I guess. He should have done that last semester."

"Missy, look." Alex pointed upward. "Can you see the robins?"

She looked up in the general direction he was pointing and shook her head. "Not really. They look like black shapes moving in the sky. How many are there? Three?" She looked back at her fiancé.

"I can see four," he answered. Then he said, "Spring has

sprung."

"Oh no, you'll never make a writer with that line, Alex."

"I don't intend to be, sweetheart. You're the writer."

She smiled and then said, "I'm really happy that our fellowship group agreed to act out my play. How long do you think it will take us to rehearse and be ready to perform?"

"I'd like to see it as a finale to the year, you know, just before final exams begin, probably about the last week of April or so," Alex replied. "Rehearsals are going better than I expected."

"That's because we have a terrific group leader."

"Yes, the Lord Himself," Alex stated quickly.

"I didn't mean him exactly," Missy admitted. "But I can't argue that one."

"Let's go this way." He steered her around a wet, muddy area in the path. "How is Zoe doing?"

"She's been all right since the last nightmare. She seems to take things in stride, so far. I think that Dr. Francis is working up the courage to have a talk with her, though. She has hinted at it with me in her office. Alex, keep praying for them."

"Of course, I will. I pray for you too, sweetheart."

"That's sweet, thank you. We all need God's loving hand."

He nodded. "Amen to that." He looked away from her, turning his attention to the terrain as they walked. They were headed back toward the main road.

"Did I tell you what Dr. Shepherd suggested?" Missy asked him.

"Your special ed teacher? No, you didn't."

"He thinks I should consider a double major. He said that the faculty evaluation of my teaching at the junior high is very favorable for special education. He also said since I love writing so much I could major in that too. Can you believe it?

"Sounds like a good idea. How many more courses do you need?"

Her eyes widened. "What? Good idea? What about extra work? I only chose the special ed course as an elective because of my counseling experience at summer camp with handicapped kids. Alex, I don't think I could handle the extra load. Five courses at a time are plenty."

"Yeah, I know. Five courses at a time is plenty for me too. Missy, what about summer school? The state division of services for the blind will help you pay for that, right?"

"How did you know they are helping me pay for my schooling?"

He looked away from her and repeated, "Well, they will, won't they?"

"Probably," she admitted. "The truth is, I was thinking about summer school this year anyway. I don't want six courses next year. But if I take a double major, I'll have to go to summer school again next summer as well. I don't know if I really want all that extra work."

Alex smiled, and then he said, "I know, but I bet you can handle it. I know you get honor grades. Besides, I'm going to be attending summer school this year myself. I want to take a couple of extra psych courses, and I don't want the extra course load either."

"Really?" She drew in a deep breath. "Alex, if it would work out, we could be together all summer too." She squeezed his arm.

He nodded. "I know."

"Ha! I bet you have been conspiring with Dr. Shepherd. You planned this, right? Alex, you still didn't answer my question. How did you know the state helps with education for the handicapped at college level?"

"Well, I, uh . . . I know a guy who has a disability, and he is getting help."

"Oh? Who is he?"

"I am sure you wouldn't know him. He's also from Milford. Missy, do you know where we are now?" He was relieved to change the subject.

She nodded while he opened the door for her to enter ahead of him. When they were inside the lobby, he asked her.

"Is Zoe going to supper with us tonight? Oh, wait a minute. I see a note in your mailbox, honey."

She made a grunting sound and went to retrieve it. She brought back a plain white envelope with her name typed on the outside of it. Tearing it open, she handed the note to Alex to read for her.

"Here, you read it to me. I didn't bring my magnifier."

Standing next to him, Missy saw the smile fade from his lips. Then he reread the note out loud, "'You will be purged, purified, and refined.' Daniel 12:10." He shook his head in denial. "I can't believe anyone would send you a note like this."

"That sounds similar to the one I got the day my skit was rejected by the junior high school committee," she commented without thinking about it.

"What? You mean, you have gotten a threatening note before this one?" He took her hand and led her toward the stairs. "I want to see it. Missy, why didn't you tell me about this before?"

"Well, I forgot. It didn't seem to be that important. Just a prank."

Alex waited in the hall while Missy went into the room to see if Zoe was there. When Missy came around the corner of the U, she saw Zoe's long profile stretched out on top of her bed.

"Are you sleeping, Zoe?"

Missy was standing close enough to her roommate to see Zoe move her head from side to side.

"No, I'm just resting. The migraine is better, but I'm still taking it easy."

Missy nodded. "It's almost suppertime. Do you mind if Alex comes in for a few minutes?"

"No. Just let me comb my hair first." Zoe got up, straightened her clothes, and went to the mirror for a look.

As she went toward the door, Missy said over her shoulder, "Don't worry. He just wants to see the other note I got before."

After closing the door when he had entered the room, she began searching in her notebooks and through her papers to find the earlier note.

"Have a seat, honey." She continued to search.

When Zoe came around the corner of Missy's desk and stepped over Alex's long stretched-out legs, she exchanged smiles with him.

"It's about time Missy told you about that note."

She went to her own desk and took the electric pot from her bottom drawer.

"Aha. Desk drawer." Missy kept hunting.

"We went for a walk out around the fairgrounds," Alex said conversationally. "I'm looking forward to bringing my bike back to school once this mud and slush dries up."

"Would you two like a cup of herbal tea before supper? I'm just getting over a migraine headache, and I'm going to have some," Zoe offered.

"Thanks, Zo. I'm thirsty after walking," Missy agreed. "I'll have cinnamon."

"I don't know." Alex was hesitant.

"Zoe has a variety of flavors," Missy told him. "You can choose."

"I guess I'll try it," he finally agreed.

"Aha. Here it is." Missy closed the bottom drawer and handed the piece of paper to her fiancé. Zoe left the room to get water for the teapot.

"What flavor do you like, Alex?"

"Missy, I think you should show these notes to the police. Has Zoe seen them?"

She turned sideways on her desk chair and nodded. "Zoe said the same thing the day of my rejection. What timing."

"Are there any more notes?" He asked.

"No, darling. I don't see what good it will do to tell the police. They can't very well trace it. I expect almost everyone on campus uses a typewriter. It's just some dumb prank."

"What's a prank?" Zoe had returned with the water.

"Missy got another one of those threatening notes in her mailbox today." Alex handed the latest one to Zoe to read for herself.

"That's crazy," she concluded.

She plugged the electric pot into the wall socket to boil the hot water for tea. Then she went to the other side of the divided room to get Styrofoam cups and plastic spoons.

Missy opened her middle desk drawer and took out containers of sugar and powdered milk.

"What flavor, Alex?"

"Missy, did you tell Alex about the Valentine?" Zoe asked when she came back around the corner.

"What Valentine?" Alex asked immediately.

"The burned rose with the unsigned card," Zoe supplied.

Alex straightened. "Melissa, what did you do with it?"

She turned to fish in her bottom drawer again. Finding the loose card, she picked it up but didn't think to retrieve the accompanying envelope with it. She handed it to him and explained briefly.

"Here's the card. I threw the nasty thing away after I opened the box downstairs in the lobby. Alex, you made me so happy that day. I didn't want to spoil it."

He studied the card as well as her face. Finally, he said quietly, "It could have been evidence, honey."

"Oh. I'm sorry. Alex, what flavor tea would you like? I'll have cinnamon, Zoe," she said to her roommate.

"I'd like to clear up the mystery of these notes," he admitted. "I think I'll try lemon if you have it, Zoe."

"We do," Zoe assured him. "I'm having peppermint this time." When the water had heated enough, Zoe poured and distributed the hot drinks.

Alex touched the hot liquid to his lips then took a sip and finally a swallow.

"Mmm. This is good. Maybe I'll get some for my room. It will be a nice change from Art's decaf."

"I offered him some," Zoe remarked, "but he wouldn't try it."

"Art has some funny ideas sometimes."

"How do you mean, funny?" Zoe asked Alex.

"I guess I should say, prejudices. He keeps to himself mostly."

"I've noticed that," Zoe agreed.

Alex turned his attention to his fair lady. "Missy, do you mind if I take these notes and the card? I want to show them to a friend of mine. Get a sort of second opinion."

"Go ahead, here." Missy stood to hand him the notes. Then she reopened the bottom drawer to get one of the envelopes with her name typed on it. The remaining two envelopes stayed in her bottom drawer.

Alex leaned forward to set his empty teacup on Missy's

desk and to take the envelope from her. He deposited the pieces of paper and put the envelope in his shirt pocket. Then he stood and stretched his arms upward, easily touching the ceiling.

Missy drained her cup and set it down. "Show-off." She teased and got up to stand in front of him. Her full height barely brought the top of her head up to his nose.

"Just right." He reached down to pat the top of her head. Smiling amiably, he turned his head to remark to Zoe. "You had better trade in your beehives for boots. It's muddy today, and my tummy says it's time to eat."

"Oh, I forgot that I still have my slippers on." Zoe went around the corner to exchange them for boots while Missy cleared away the accessories and unplugged the hot water pot.

On the following Tuesday, Missy and Zoe were walking to Parker House for a meeting with Dr. Francis.

"I wonder why she specifically asked me to wear my necklace," Zoe wondered out loud. "I hope it doesn't bring me bad luck." Zoe had chosen to wear her green dress that clearly accented the beehive around her neck and her green eyes.

"Maybe she has one like it." Missy tried to choose her words carefully.

"I doubt it," Zoe countered.

"Zoe, try to keep an open mind. She probably has a reason."

Zoe's countenance fell and her mouth dropped open in surprise when she entered Dr. Francis' office and saw an exact duplicate of her own necklace hanging around the older woman's neck.

"I don't believe it. Where did you get that, Dr. Francis? Sister Ruth at the orphanage told me that my mother had the only other one."

"Sit down, Zoe, and I'll try to explain. Missy, would you close the door please?" Dr. Francis waited until Missy had complied and sat back down beside her roommate before continuing. "You see, Zoe, my grandmother, Rose Babette, used to make ceramic crafts as a hobby. She lived with my parents and me while I was growing up. She knew of my fear of bees because I am allergic to their stings. She made me a necklace of a beehive to help me cope. It reminded me of her strength and love. I was an only child. Anyway, during my second year of high school, I . . ."

Barbara's voice broke, and she paused in midsentence. She leaned forward in her desk chair, seemingly searching for words. After a glance at Missy, she swallowed and then continued.

"When I was raped, my grandmother made another necklace, an exact duplicate, for my baby, for my daughter, when she was born." Her voice caught, and she lost the battle she was having with tears. In shaky broken sobs, she continued. "Please try to understand. I . . . I have the birth certificate here to prove it and a baby picture in my locket along with my grandmother's picture." She rested her elbows on top of her desk and clasped her hands together. "I was only fifteen, still a child myself. I just couldn't handle the responsibility of raising a . . . another person. Zoe, I know it will take time. Please try . . . try to forgive me for . . . for abandoning you. I thought adoption was the best solution at that time. I am your mother, Zoe."

Barbara was now sobbing openly. Her forehead rested against her clenched hands, which supported the weight of her long-held guilt.

"No. I don't believe it." Zoe stared at the document on the desk and the broken woman who was sitting behind it.

Missy was praying silently with hands folded in her lap.

Zoe's voice shook as anger, rage, resentment, and confusion fought for dominance within.

"Why? How? How could you have given up your own child?"

"Here, I'll show you . . . I have your baby picture, and . . ." Barbara's voice trailed off as she released her hands to remove the necklace.

She fumbled with the tiny clasp with cold, trembling fingers. When she had finally succeeded in opening the shell, she placed it on the desk for Zoe to examine.

Zoe picked up the open piece of jewelry. She gasped when she saw the apparition from her dream smiling at her from the photo within it. Zoe clamped it shut and threw the object across the desk as if it were a hot ember. Barbara retrieved it on a slide as it was headed for the edge.

Zoe, who had stood, was now backing toward the door. Her face had gone pale, and her hands were trembling.

Her voice had gone shrill with hysteria as she blurted out, "If this is your idea of a cruel joke, I don't like it one bit. That woman is the ghost in my nightmare. You can't fool me. I'm getting out of here."

Zoe turned to open the office door and dart through. It slammed following her hasty exit.

"Barbara, may I see the pictures?" Missy asked. "It's going to take time for her to accept this. Give her some time to calm down."

Again the older woman opened the locket and this time handed it to Missy. Under magnification, Missy first looked at the baby picture then at a full-length view of an elderly woman in a deep-rose-colored robe. The woman was smiling. Missy explained the reality of Zoe's dream to Barbara.

Then she added, "I guess I should have prepared you beforehand, Barbara. I'm sorry. Apparently, your grandmother's picture and your parents' house have brought Zoe's nightmare into reality.

Dr. Francis took the locket back and hung it around her neck again. She drew in a shaky breath, trying to regain her composure.

"Zoe was born in that house."

"What? She told me she was born in Manchester," Missy said.

"My parents took us to Manchester to have us checked out in a city hospital away from small-town talk. I thought it would be easier to have her placed in the orphanage there. I thought she would be adopted. When I left her with Sister Ruth, I also left the necklace for her. I guess I wanted her to have some family tie even if it was anonymous to her. The locket was a unique keepsake symbol. Missy, shouldn't you go after her?"

Missy nodded and stood. "I just wanted to be sure you were all right before I left."

"Yes. Thank you. I'll be praying for both of us."

Stepping out into the sweet spring afternoon air, Missy looked for her roommate's green dress color as she walked. She was turning around, trying to look around, when she tripped over an obstacle. With a surprised exclamation, she looked into the frowning features of a brown-haired male student. She had tripped over his feet as he had approached from behind her. She opened her mouth to apologize, but he spoke first.

"Hey, look where you're going." Then he cursed her and pushed past her to walk away.

She did not recognize the brown-haired young man, but his voice sounded familiar. She stood still, thinking, trying to place it. His rudeness stood out in her mind. Maybe it had been at the dining commons where she had heard him speak. She seemed to recall an impatient male voice in line behind her at times.

"Melissa." He waited for her to recognize him.

Missy jumped, startled by the deep, nasal-sounding voice that now intruded upon her thoughts. It came from her left.

"Art. I didn't see you there."

He stuck a long, slim finger up in front of her nose. "You wait, Melissa. Your time is coming. You'll get what you deserve. Mark my words."

"Art, I don't understand. Have you seen Zoe?"

"Yes, I've seen Zoe. She is going to change, and then we are going for a walk. I should have known that you would have something to do with upsetting her. She ran right into me a few minutes ago."

"I'm afraid it is something she had to know sooner or later. Hopefully time will heal her hurt. I'll walk back to the dorm with you if you don't mind." Missy hurried to keep up her stride with him. "Did Alex tell y—"

"Ya, he told me," Art interrupted her with a short tone of voice. "It won't last, old maid. Eventually, he will see through you."

"Art, who do you think I am? I don't understand you."

"No matter, Melissa. Things will work out in time."

Both were silent as they walked across the street and up the walk to Falcon Hall.

"I'll tell Zoe you're waiting." Missy was relieved to part company with him in the lobby and head up the stairs.

His eyes narrowed as he watched her ascend the steps. Then, automatically, he took a piece of candy from his shirt pocket. Unwrapping the deep-yellow cellophane, he popped the piece of butterscotch in his mouth and let the wrapper fall to the floor.

"Zoe," Missy called as she entered their room. Turning the corner by her desk, she found her roommate dressing. She saw the rumpled heap of green-and-white clothing on Zoe's bed.

"You already knew, didn't you?"

"Yes, Zo. Dr. Francis told me when I was almost raped. She wanted to be certain that it really was you before she worked up the courage to talk to you about it. She has been living with hurt and guilt for a long time."

"So what am I supposed to do? Forgive and forget? Well, I can't do that, and if that is what being a Christian is all about, I don't want any part of that either. Don't wait for me to go to supper, and don't wait up for me. I don't know when I'll come back."

"Want me to hang up your dress?"

"I don't care."

Bang. The door slammed behind her.

Missy exchanged her skirt and top for jeans and a bright-red turtleneck sweater. Mechanically, she put her and Zoe's clothes away. When she was passing the bureau section that separated their closets, she saw a brown lump on its flat surface. Reaching out to touch it, she realized that it was Zoe's beehive necklace. She opened Zoe's top bureau drawer, found its small box, and placed the trinket inside. Then she closed the drawer after replacing the box.

Missy then went to her closet to get her red parka. She knew it would be cool when the sun went down. She hoped that she and Alex could study together. She didn't want to be alone, not when she had friends who were hurting.

The time she waited in the lobby for her fiancé seemed longer than it actually was to her. Relief surged through her like electricity when she heard Alex's pleasant greeting. She went to hug him.

"Mmm. I could get used to this kind of treatment," he told her.

"I'm so glad to see you, darling. Zoe and I had a meeting with Dr. Francis a little while ago."

"Oh, I see. Zoe didn't take it very well, huh? Don't feel guilty, honey. It wasn't your fault."

Missy sighed and relaxed in his embrace. His fingers caressed the long strands of her hair with gentle assurance. She lifted her head to look at him.

"Alex, what are you doing after supper tonight?"

"Probably not what I'd like to be doing." He smiled.

She ignored the implication. "Alex, could we study together? I don't want to be alone."

"Of course we can."

She smiled and released her embrace to take his arm as they turned to exit the building and walk to the dining commons.

"Alex, I love you."

Later that night, Missy was asleep. She didn't hear Zoe's insistent pounding on the door, which she had left unlocked. She also slept through the sound of Zoe's desk chair squealing as Zoe staggered against it and pushed it along the floor. She had finally managed to open the door.

"Missssey, you here?" Zoe's words were slurred.

She reached out to steady herself by holding on to the desktop. Then Zoe made a dash for her bed. After lying still for a while, Zoe rolled over to slowly stand and change into her night clothes. Then she got back into bed. Sleep came quickly.

Startled by the shriek of her alarm clock, Missy bolted upright in bed and then reached to silence it.

"I thought it was the fire alarm for a minute. Zoe, you here?"

Her roommate moaned and plopped her pillow over her face.

Missy got up quietly and padded over to the other bed. "Are you sick?"

"Hangover."

"Okay," Missy whispered.

When Missy stepped outside into the early spring dawn on Friday morning, the wind whipped her ponytail around like the scorn of a bullwhip to strike her in the face. She looked upward while waiting for Alex. The sky betrayed its fickleness with clusters of white and yellow-gray all in motion against a backdrop of blue. Her mood seemed to be caught up in the ferocity of the atmosphere as a headache began to pound for notice.

"Hi, honey. What are you looking at?"

Missy lowered her gaze, recognizing Alex's soft, soothing voice, and turned her head to look at him. She could not see his wistful expression.

She replied thoughtfully, "The sky looks angry this morning." She hugged him with one arm and clutched her books and tape recorder to her stomach with the other.

"Yeah, the air is menacingly warm," he agreed. "It's stirring up to a storm, no doubt. Have you gotten any mail lately?"

Missy shrugged. "Don't know. I haven't looked. Why?"

He slid an arm around her waist, and they began to move down the walk toward the street. "Just wondered. Missy, Pete and I both think you should show these notes to the police. I have them with me. Remind me to give them back to you at breakfast."

"Alex, it's probably just a cruel joke. People who have handicaps deal with ridicule all the time. Some people don't want to take the time and effort to understand the person who has a disability. Besides, the police can't do anything about notes."

"Well then, do it for me, Missy. What if they are a threat?"

She was silent for a few moments. Finally, she agreed. "I guess I can stop by the police station on my way back from school this afternoon. Thank God it's Friday. It will be a busy day, and I'm getting a headache already."

He reached up to gently yank on her ponytail and then rested his hand on her shoulder. "You know, it seems as if we're married already. I only get to see you at meals and a couple of evenings maybe."

"Better get used to it. It will probably be this way when we are married and working."

"Oh. You don't want to stay at home?" he asked her.

"Two incomes are better than one, honey."

When they entered the dining commons and had taken their trays, he read the breakfast menu for her. Once they were seated, he asked her how Zoe was doing.

Missy shook her head. "She is taking it hard. We haven't spoken much since our meeting with Dr. Francis. Alex, maybe Zoe would be more open if she talked to you. We haven't been getting along too well lately." She picked at her scrambled eggs.

"What's the matter, Missy?" he asked when he saw her frown.

She was fishing in her purse. "Headache." Finding it, she took out a small bottle of aspirin and removed two pills from the bottle. Then she put the bottle back in her purse.

Alex stood. "I'll get you some milk. It'll go down better with that than tea."

She smiled as he left the table. Silently, she thanked God for His love and caring, also for Alex's love. Then she prayed for her roommate and for wisdom to help Zoe sort out her feelings. Soon Alex returned with her drink and some more toast. She thanked him and took her pills.

Afterward she said, "Alex, you have got to talk to Art. I don't understand why he continually accuses me of being a meddling old maid."

Alex shook his head. "He's just set in his narrow-minded way, and he won't change. You'd better eat faster if you want to finish in time for your eight-o'clock class."

She rubbed her hand across her forehead and then took a larger bite of food.

"Missy, can you cook?"

She looked surprised at his question. She smiled and then answered, "Of course I can cook. My father says I cook better than my mother sometimes."

They continued their bantering through the remainder of the meal. Afterward, when they had gone outside to part company, Alex put a restraining hand on her shoulder.

"Missy, be careful."

Sensing the serious tone in his voice, she held her tongue and gave him a quick kiss instead.

"I will, darling."

When Missy returned to her room that afternoon, she opened the door cautiously. Peering inside, she was relieved to see Zoe sitting at her desk sipping tea with a book open in front of her. Missy smiled and stepped inside to close the door. She put her own books down on her desk and sat sideways in her chair.

"Studying diligently?" she asked Zoe.

Zoe sighed. "Not really. Hey, I'm sorry I gave you such a hard time the other day. I didn't mean to take my problems out on you."

Missy smiled and nodded. "I know. You feeling better?"

"I guess so. I just feel angry."

"It will take time to heal. Oh, by the way, I wanted to ask

you if you are still going to Todd's lecture tonight?"

"Does it really matter now? The danger was last semester. The guy was caught. Want some tea?" She held the box of tea bags out to Missy.

Missy held the box close to her face to see which flavor she wanted. "That sounds good. I still have a headache from this morning. Any cinnamon left?" Finally, she pulled up the right item and put the box down. "Zoe, I would like you to go with me tonight. Alex will be busy helping Todd with his presentation. I expect it will be down pouring rain too by then. The air is hot and heavy for a thunder boomer." She set her teacup on the desk and gestured for Zoe to pour.

"I should have known. Seasonal changes always bring migraines. Where have you been anyway? Aren't you later today?"

Missy nodded and then sipped her tea. She put her cup down to explain. "I went to the police with my lovely notes. They said there isn't anything they can do until a crime has been committed. Now I can tell Alex, 'I told you so.'" But she did not smile.

"Missy, do you think that someone is really out to get you?"

Missy shook her head. "No, but Alex was concerned. Speaking of this matter, I guess I'll go check my mailbox. I'll be right back."

Zoe took their cups to the bathroom to wash them while Missy was gone. When Missy returned, Zoe had already gotten her raincoat out for her and was ready to go to supper. Missy handed Zoe the folded piece of paper and sat down, anticipating the hateful remarks.

Zoe read, "'How beautiful is your love my bride . . . How much better is your love than wine.'" Missy didn't see Zoe's eyebrows arch in a gesture of bewilderment. She continued to read, "'And the fragrance of your oils than all kinds of spices.' Song of Solomon 4:10." Zoe shook her head.

"Well, is it signed?" Excitement danced in Missy's voice.

"Whom do you think?" Zoe replied. "I think the nasty ones make more sense."

"So that's why Alex wanted me to check my mail this morning."

"It's signed . . ."

Missy grabbed at the piece of paper. In response, Zoe held it up higher.

"Let me see."

After a couple of attempts, Missy snatched the piece of paper. With her magnifying glass, she read "Passionately yours, Alex."

Missy shook her head and smiled. Folding the note, she put in in her bottom drawer along with the nasty ones.

She and Zoe stepped out into the hall and closed the now-locked door.

"Let's go this way." Zoe turned right to go down the stairs to the nearest side exit door. "I'll see Alex if he is coming up the walk," Zoe assured her friend. "The lobby has a glass front, so he can see us also from inside."

As they started out toward the hall door exit, Missy ran her hand across the glass casing of the square compartment that housed the fire extinguisher in the wall.

"I wonder when we will have a fire drill this semester?"

"Sh. It will probably be tonight with Mr. Francis's lecture," Zoe answered.

Missy nodded as she mentally counted steps on her way down.

Once outside, the humidity in the air weighed heavily upon them like the threat of an imminent explosion.

"The sky looks mean," Missy commented as she looked up into a gray–black overcast. "The air feels heavy too."

Zoe waved to Alex, who was crossing the street headed in their direction. "With our luck, the downpour will start while we're eating in the dining commons. Here comes Alex," Zoe told her roommate.

It did. The girls were dismayed to return to their room and find a power outage from a lightning strike during their absence. By the time they left with Laurie and Susan to attend the lecture, however, the electricity in the dorm had been restored back to normal.

Missy was surprised that Art greeted them with a smile when the little group of girls entered the science building lecture hall.

"Missy, this is the best seat in the house if you want to keep up with the lecture tonight."

Art gestured toward the corner seat in the front row along the outside wall. The girls stepped up onto the platform to take seats along the front row with Missy on the end as Art had suggested. The seating was arranged in a semicircular pattern ascending up steps at each row level toward the back of the room.

"Strange for him to go out of his way to be nice," Laurie muttered to Zoe, who was sitting beside Missy.

"He can be nice when he wants to," Zoe replied.

Missy tapped Zoe's arm. "What is Art doing?"

"Looks like he is checking the wiring on the floor in front of us," Zoe answered. "Can you see the easel in front?" Zoe pointed.

Recognizing a large, white rectangle, Missy nodded.

The girls, as well as the other spectators, talked quietly while waiting for the lecture to begin. No one noticed that one back leg of Missy's metal chair had an extension cord wire wrapped around it at the bottom. The cord was plugged into a nearby wall socket close to the floor. As time passed, the chair leg began to cut into the cord as Missy shifted positions, waiting for the lecture to begin.

"Why don't they start?" Susan asked. "It's well after eight o'clock."

Static crackled from the microphone, which was held by a tall blond man. Missy recognized Alex's voice when he apologized for the delay and asked for patience. He said that Mr. Francis must have been unavoidably detained and had not yet arrived.

Art, carrying several items, was walking toward the girls.

"I thought you girls might like something to drink while waiting." He smiled as he handed each of the four a soft drink can from the vending machine in the hall. "Don't know what is keeping our guest speaker."

When he finished speaking, Art made a sweeping gesture with his arms. As his right arm rose, he hit the opened can in Missy's hand. The aluminum container clinked to the carpet, spilling its liquid contents.

Missy screamed as her body was jolted by shocking electrical current. Sparks from the severed wire flashed and danced merrily, starting a small fire at the corner of the upturned thin carpet.

14

Running Scared

Within seconds, Alex had quenched the fire before it had begun to gather fuel. As the vapors from the fire extinguisher began to dissolve, the guest lecturer walked into the auditorium.

"Missy."

The warmth of Alex's touch seemed to restore life to her rigid, startled body. Her hand reached for his. She held on to his reassuring strength for a moment. Finally, she spoke.

"Thank you, darling. I'm all right."

Alex released her to examine her chair. Much of the spilled liquid had been absorbed by her slacks and sweater while the remainder lay in an innocent puddle on the wooden platform. It dripped slowly to the carpet below.

"What on earth happened?" Todd asked.

"You could say that Missy had a shocking experience," Pete explained and pointed to the severed wire now lying between the legs of Missy's abandoned chair. "Here, see, the chair leg must have been cutting into the extension cord."

"I didn't see that," Zoe exclaimed. "Art was just here

checking the wiring too. I bet he didn't even notice it either."

"Looks as if you've had your lesson already," Todd said. "I was delayed by rainy weather coming back from business."

"Where is Art anyway?" Alex asked.

"I think he went to put the fire extinguisher back," Zoe supplied. "Oh, here he comes."

Art and another student returned with a mop and bucket to wipe up the mess under Missy's chair. Art held out another can of drink to Missy, but she was shaking her head no.

"Take it as my apology," Art insisted. "I didn't mean to knock that drink out of your hand. How did that wire get cut?"

"My chair leg was cutting into it, but no one saw it," Missy said. Then she thanked him for the drink.

When the liquid on the floor had been sopped up and the broken cord had been replaced and repositioned, Alex sat in Missy's chair. Nothing happened.

"You can sit down now, honey. It is safe."

Todd began his lecture forty-five minutes late. He had made it a point to speak to Alex alone first. They made arrangements for a meeting to compare notes.

Alex and Missy spent most of their waking hours together that weekend, talking, studying, and enjoying each other's company. Alex's protective instincts were almost as strong as his male masculinity, and he wrestled with his emotions to keep them under his control.

Todd had privately insisted on treating Alex to lunch at the Student Union coffee shop on Monday. When the day arrived, the two of them sat at a rear corner table for their discussion.

"Alex, I don't want to alarm you, but judging from what you've told me about Missy's nasty notes and now this latest incident, it seems to me that someone is targeting her deliberately."

Alex nodded slowly and replaced his teacup on the saucer. "I know. I just didn't want to believe it myself. Who in the world would want to hurt her?"

"I was going to ask you that question, old chap." Todd bit into his sandwich.

Alex shook his head. "Aw, Todd, I don't know. I love her." He picked up his spoon and stirred his tea again.

"Well, if it isn't her exactly, then maybe it's something about her," Todd persisted. "We need a clue."

"Mmm." Alex made a sound of realization while chewing his chicken salad sandwich. When he had finished his bite, he explained, "There is one thing. Art has this stupid prejudice about people who have handicaps, and he is always making remarks about Missy, but he is a Christian. I don't think he could be that malicious, Todd."

"Hmm. It can't hurt to run a background check on him anyway. Maybe someone else on campus shares his prejudices. Where is he from?"

Alex thought for a moment. "Let's see. He said he transferred from, uh, Troy, NY, I think."

Todd nodded. "Now, how about some dessert, Alex? I am going to have pie, I think."

"All right. You can order me a dish of butterscotch pudding and another cup of tea. I'll be right back."

"Where are you going?"

"To the bathroom to take my medication." The words just slid out naturally. Alex frowned, waiting for the logical question.

"Oh." Todd hesitated momentarily then he asked it. "What for?"

"I have a condition that is controlled by medication." Alex turned to walk away and muttered to himself, "When the doctors find the right medication."

When Alex returned, his dessert was waiting for him.

Todd set his coffee cup down and began a different conversation.

"By the way, Alex, the Burns will be moving back into their house next weekend. Carol and Dennis would like you chaps to come out and visit again and maybe help us move them. They've accumulated more belongings as time passed. You know what I mean."

Alex nodded. "Sure. Missy and I will come. This is good pudding."

"Barbara would like you and Missy to try to persuade Zoe to come also. I know that's a tall order," Todd admitted.

"You said a mouthful. All we can do is try. It might be good therapy to get her and Barbara to talk it out, but I don't really know. We'll see."

Todd murmured his thanks and sipped his coffee.

Alex held the spoon in his mouth for a moment. He was remembering another time when he had taken Missy out for pudding and they had gone along with Pete after Joe's house fire. It seemed as if years had passed since then, but it had only been four months. Alex smiled as he replaced his spoon in the now–empty dish.

"It's kinda hard to believe that I'm going to be married, Todd. I know that Missy is right for me though. It's God's design."

"Alex, my friend, time and trials are true tests of love."

"Well, we're certainly passing the trials test so far."

The following Saturday morning, Carol Babette greeted the little group at the door. Zoe had agreed to go but with obvious reluctance. When she stepped inside the wide hallway entrance and saw the photographs of various individuals on the ivory-colored walls, the long, high archway above them, and the spiral staircase with the brown-and-beige patchwork carpeting—her nightmare became a reality!

"I . . . I . . . can't stay here!" Her voice faltered and rose in heightened fear as her eyes darted in all directions. She turned to fiddle with the handle of the heavy steel door. Finally succeeding in opening it, she fled outside, running down the walkway.

Alex went after her. "Zoe, where will you go? We're way out of town."

"Let go of me, Alex! You don't understand!"

He was still grasping her wrist. "Wait. Talk to me, Zoe. Tell me what is wrong. Let me help you."

Her eyes showed like glass as tears of fear welled up in them to spill out in streams. Alex put his arms around her, trying to comfort her. He let her cry on his shoulder. Oddly, there was no torrent of emotion raging within him like he always felt when he held Missy. There was no aching longing, no jubilant excitement, no emotion, really, except compassion and concern. He was just comforting another human being.

Finally, Zoe calmed enough to speak. "Alex, the ghost is on the wall. I can't go back in there."

Had she gone completely mad and lost all touch with reality? "Zoe, that makes no sense at all. Please explain yourself."

She lifted her head and her hands to wipe her eyes. Alex still held onto her shoulders. "Surely Missy has told you about the nightmare that I keep having over and over again? Well, here it is, right here inside this house. The ghost who appears in my dream and says 'Do what you must do' is in one of those pictures on the wall. Please—don't make me go back in there! I . . . I just can't face it!"

Recollection dawned in Alex's memory. No wonder she was

so frightened.

"Zoe, listen to me." He paused patiently. "Don't you want to be rid of this fearful dream?"

She nodded silently.

"Then you have to face up to it. Stand up to your fear. We can help you, Zoe. You are not alone," he assured her.

"I ... I ... don't know ..."

"You will probably find that there is a logical explanation."

Her expression betrayed her doubt, but she was willing to trust Alex. She sighed shakily and began to take slow steps back toward the house. Alex walked with her with his arm around her waist for reassurance.

When they stepped back inside, Carol and Missy were the only people in the wide hallway. Seeing Alex's questioning look, Carol told them that the others had gone to help the Burns with their things on the first trip. They all would be back later.

"Now, Zoe, can you point out the picture that frightens you? Maybe Carol can tell you who it is." Alex's arm still held her reassuringly.

Zoe pointed to the portrait. Her face was as white as the woman's hair in the picture. She looked away.

"That was Dennis's mother, Barbara's grandmother," Carol said.

"*Was.*" Zoe choked on the word. "She is the ghost in my dream."

"Oh no," Missy breathed as Zoe's vivid description suddenly flashed in her memory.

"It's all right," Alex said firmly. "Now, Zoe, what else did you see in your dream? Take your time."

"The hall entrance, the spiral staircase, the woman was in the kitchen. She was f-f-floating ... above the kitchen table ... and there was water boiling on the stove and white towels on the counter, but there was no one else there."

"Did you go upstairs in your dream?" Missy asked with deliberate calm in her voice.

"Oh, yes. I was upstairs at first. There was a baby crying—wailing—and shadows. There were shadowy, shapeless figures. They were whispering God knows what. I couldn't understand the words ... I couldn't hear them. They were muffled."

"A baby crying," Carol repeated. "Zoe, you were born here, in this house. We took you to Manchester the same day. We wanted to be sure you were healthy."

Zoe felt the color flee from her features as weakness approached. "I ... I think I need to sit down."

When Alex realized that Missy didn't see the look he was giving her, he spoke her name.

Missy came to the aid of her friend while Carol led them into the large living room to sit.

"Zoe," Alex continued in a clear but patient tone of voice, "once you learn to understand what you were afraid of, you can learn to cope with it."

"I ... I ... hope so, Alex." Zoe replied in a shaky voice.

15

The Burning Pain

By the time the others had returned from their first moving trip, Zoe had regained enough composure to aid in the task. She was grateful for Ashley's bubbly chatter as a much-needed diversion.

In spite of her attempted cheerfulness, Alex understood the strain between her and Barbara. Whenever Barbara looked in Zoe's direction, Alex saw her turn away. If Barbara happened to stand near Zoe, she would move to another spot.

When the move was completed, Carol invited everyone to stay for a hardy meal after such hard work. Now they were all seated in the large living room at the Babettes' home.

"I want to thank all of you for your help," Joe said with sincerity. It could have taken days. I ain't used to makin' speeches, but I'll never forget this, thank you—all of you."

"Ya, me too," Ashley said. She bounded across the patchwork carpet to sit on the floor in front of Missy.

"Ashley, may I have some of that energy?" Zoe asked.

Ashley giggled.

"As long as everyone is here," Alex began, "I think this is as good a time as any to make our announcement." He glanced at Missy and squeezed her hand that he had been holding. "Missy and I are engaged to be married."

"Oh, that's wonderful news." Barbara smiled warmly at her husband.

He grinned and turned toward Alex and Missy to say teasingly, "Why in the world would you want to go and do that?"

Joe nodded, but his expression remained sober.

Carol and Dennis also exchanged meaningful glances, and they added their congratulations.

"Missy, can I be a bridesmaid?" Ashley asked.

"That is for the bride to choose, Ashley," Barbara corrected her.

"It's all right," Missy said. "Actually, I had hoped you would be my flower girl."

"Really? Can I, Grandpa?"

"Yes, you may. Now, when is this event to take place?"

"Ah, we haven't exactly decided yet," Missy told Joe.

"If you folks will excuse me, I'll tend to supper." Carol got up to leave the room.

"Come with me, Ashley." Barbara stood also. "Maybe we can help my mother with supper. All right?"

"Okay." She got up and skipped agreeably out of the room.

Alex saw Zoe's features relax a little after Barbara had left the room. He watched her lean a little less rigidly against the back of her easy chair.

Dennis got up to stoke the fire in the fireplace.

"Zoe, are you feeling a little better now?" Missy asked.

"I guess a little. Thanks."

"We are proud of your courage, Zoe," Alex added.

A sudden shriek from across the hall brought the men to

their feet and running. Alex and Todd were the first to arrive on the scene. Seeing Barbara's distress, Todd swiftly scooped her up in his arms to carry her to the car and transport her to the Iandale Hospital.

"I didn't mean to. I'm sorry. I'm sorry," Ashley cried hysterically in between her wailing.

When he first entered the kitchen, Alex had found Barbara agonized with pain from the hot grease that had spilled out of the frying pan, which was now lying overturned on the linoleum. Flames had flared around the burner of the stove, which Carol had just turned off.

Now Alex took Ashley's arm and led her toward the door of the kitchen.

"Ashley, go to Missy in the other room."

Alex then turned to assist the other men in extinguishing the fire. Afterward Carol deposited the frying pan in the sink and began to clean up the floor.

Missy hugged Ashley, trying to comfort and quiet her. Zoe, who had seen Todd carry Barbara from the house and had briefly seen the flames from the kitchen, described to Missy what was happening. Both had heard Ashley's wailing cries. When Ashley had calmed enough to speak, Missy asked her what had happened.

Ashley was breathless as her words came fast.

"Auntie Carol just took all the hamburgers out of the frying pan when I accidentally hit the handle and it fell on the floor. The hot stuff spilled all over Auntie Barbara and all over the place, and then there was fire on top of the stove. I didn't mean to do it!"

Missy hugged her tightly as she continued to cry. "It was an accident, Ashley. Everyone knows that, even Auntie Barbara."

"It could have been any one of us who hit that handle." Zoe

tried to sound reassuring as she rubbed Ashley's trembling back.

Ashley looked up at Missy. "If I was Auntie Barbara, I would be awful mad at me."

Missy shook her head and then answered, "Don't worry. Uncle Todd will make sure she gets the best treatment. He has already taken her to the hospital."

Once the mess in the kitchen had been cleaned up, Carol insisted that they all eat together anyway. During the meal, Todd called to say that his wife was being treated for second-degree burns and would be kept for observation.

"I want to go to the hospital to see her as soon as we can."

"Of course we will, honey," Alex agreed.

Zoe was silent.

On their way to church the following morning, Missy, Alex, and a reluctant Zoe stopped briefly at the hospital to see Barbara. Todd would be taking her home later that day.

"Well, we won't have creative writing class for a few days," Missy said as they walked to church together.

"No one should have that much pain," Zoe said.

"Pain takes many forms," Alex observed.

"I know. But she looked awful," Zoe stated. "I feel awful too. I don't think I should be going to church with you after what I said about not wanting to be Christian anymore."

"You're forgetting, Zoe. God loves you unconditionally, no matter what your mood," Alex reminded her.

"Yeah? Then how come I feel so uncomfortable?"

"That's the conviction of the Holy Spirit," Missy added.

"In other words," Alex explained, "your conscience is telling you that there is something not right between you and God. It needs to be confessed and forgiven."

"Why does it have to be so personal?"

"Because your commitment to Christ is personal. It is between you and Him alone," Missy answered.

After church, Zoe came out even angrier. "Personal, ha. I think you two had it set up with the preacher. Preaching on bitterness and unforgiveness, it's as if he were speaking just to me."

Missy put a hand on her friend's arm. "Zoe, he had no idea what your problems are. We didn't know ahead of time what the sermon would be about. It is the conviction of the Holy Spirit that is making you uncomfortable."

"You mean, God is trying to tell me something?"

"Exactly," Alex agreed. "Now let's go get some lunch."

One afternoon when Missy had returned from school teaching, Sue called her over to the front desk.

"Missy, I saw a guy put a letter in your mailbox today. I thought you might want to know since several people have asked me if I've seen anyone. This is the first time that I have."

"Oh, really? Do you know who he was, Sue?"

Sue went to the box to get Missy's letter and came back shaking her head.

"I can't place him although I know I've seen him around. He has brown hair, he's not as tall as Alex and not as muscular either." Sue smiled and then asked, "Do you know him?"

Missy shook her head. "I might be able to recognize his voice, but not a face. I'll have to tell Alex about this when he comes." She tore open the envelope with mounting dread. Taking out her magnifier, she read, "An ungodly witness scorneth judgment." She stuffed the note in her purse. "Terrific."

"What's terrific?"

Missy turned to face her fiancé. Her expression clearly showed disdain.

"Hi, honey. Read any good Bible verses lately, like Proverbs

19:28?" She handed him the newest note.

Alex read it quickly and shook his head. His expression said that he didn't want to believe what was happening. When he looked up, Sue was the first to speak.

"Judging from your expression, I gather it isn't good news. Alex, I saw the guy who put that in Missy's mailbox."

"Bless you, Sue" Alex exclaimed.

Sue held up a hand. "Now, wait a minute. I don't know him, but I probably could recognize him again. He had brown hair, he wasn't as tall as you or as nicely built."

Alex looked away as he thought over the description. Finally, he replied, "The only person I can think of is Art's science lab partner, Charlie Harris."

"You know him then?" Missy asked.

"Not really, but I think it's about time we got acquainted."

It was not difficult for Alex to corner Charlie Harris by way of knowing his roommate's class schedule. Alex indicated the direction as they began to walk side by side.

"I need to talk to you, Charlie, and I know you don't have another class right away," Alex began.

"Whatcha want with me?"

"Do you know my fiancé, Missy Sanders?"

Charlie shrugged his shoulders silently.

"Well then, you know who she is, don't you?" Alex persisted.

"Ya, sure. Everybody knows who the blind girl is. I try to stay out of her way." Again he shrugged his shoulders. "Can't always."

Alex pointed toward the gym as they crossed the street. "What do you mean, 'Can't always,' Charlie?" Alex repeated his phrase.

"Ida know. She ran right into me a couple of times."

"Where?"

"Ida know, around campus, like in the dining hall and other places. One time it was right outside the English department building, and I almost never go there if I can help it. English freshman year was enough. So I try to stay out of her way."

"Are there any courses you do like?" Alex asked. "What are you doing here, anyway, if you don't like school that much?" Alex held the door open while the shorter man pushed his way through first. Alex indicated the direction as they continued to walk. He remained silent, waiting for Charlie to answer him.

"I like usin' my hands, see, buildin' things. Give me a set o' plans, a map, a diagram, an idea even, but don't ask me to conjugate verbs and that stuff. I like puzzles and numbers. They make sense to me."

"Why did you continue going to school then?"

"Because of my old man mostly. He says he wants at least one of us to get a good education, and I am the oldest. Lucky me, ha?"

"Work out much?" Alex asked briefly as they went into the weight room.

Charlie shook his head. "Hey, what did you bring me here for anyway? I got things to do."

"What things?" Alex removed a steel bar from its slot to add weights to it.

"Studyin'."

"Don't we all?" Alex paused to lift the bar then came to the point after lowering it again. "I want to know why you were putting a note in my fiancé's mailbox."

"What makes you think I did that?" Charlie asked.

"You were seen."

"By who?"

"By whom," Alex corrected. He said no more but continued

to lift the weighted bar several times before replacing it in its slot.

"Who saw me? I mean . . . I don't know nothin'."

"Well then," Alex folded his arms across his chest, "where did you get the note?"

Charlie began to fumble with a mechanism adjustment on the nearby universal gym. He was giving it his undivided attention for a time. Finally, he spoke briefly.

"Found it."

"What?" Alex had been calculating his questions and wasn't anticipating this answer.

"I found it." He repeated. "I mean, it was the Good Samaritan thing to do, wasn't it?"

"I don't understand what you are saying."

"I found this envelope with her name on it lyin' on the counter in the science lab, so I took it and dropped it off."

"Ever done this before?" Alex was giving Charlie the full benefit of his attention now.

Charlie let go of the mechanism and shrugged his shoulders again. "Maybe," he said simply.

"Where do these notes come from?" Alex asked.

"Ida know."

"How do they get left in the science lab?" Alex tried another approach.

Charlie shook his head. "Don't ask me."

Alex stepped toward the other man. Charlie began to back up, but the machine stopped his regression. Alex stood directly in front of him and took ahold of his shirt.

"Hey, now wait a minute. I told ya, I don't know nothin' okay?" Charlie's face paled. "Besides, she ain't worth it, this fuss you're makin'."

"Why do you say that?" Alex's voice rose sharply.

"There are plenty of girls around here. Why go after one that is like that? That's all."

"Like what?" Alex asked.

"You know, handicapped."

"You got something against people who have handicaps?" Alex's face began to color with anger.

Charlie shook his head.

"You sure?" Alex persisted. "You're beginning to sound like Art Wills."

Charlie nodded.

"Tell you what," Alex released his grip, "if you get another note . . ."

Charlie nodded obediently. He wanted Alex to know that he had his full attention now.

". . . I want it. You bring it to me. Understand?"

"Sure, Alex."

"And don't leave it with Art or someone else. You be the Good Samaritan and deliver it personally. Got it?"

Charlie was nodding fervently. "Okay. I will."

Alex turned and strode out of the room.

Later Alex recapped his conversation with Charlie while he walked across campus with his best friend Pete.

"Aw, Pete, I thought we had a clue," he concluded. "I just can't believe it."

"So you believe his story then?" Pete asked.

"I don't know." Frustration edged Alex's voice. "It sounds strange. I mean, to be an errand boy and not know for whom? He says he's found a couple of sealed envelopes lying around in the lab after class and was just doing a good deed by delivering them to the addressee."

"How did he know that Missy lives in Falcon Hall?" Pete asked. "It's not the only girls' dorm on campus."

"That's a good question, Pete. I think I'll let you do all the interrogating from now on. Did I tell you that Missy threw out the evidence? I'll bet that burned rose had plenty of fingerprints on it. What was she thinking?"

"Probably how ugly and revolting it looked," Pete said. "It's natural to want to get rid of something disgusting."

"Yeah," Alex agreed, "but things are looking worse, not better."

16

Tandemonium

March yielded to April, and spring erased all traces of winter. Missy went to change into jeans and a short-sleeved top as Alex had instructed her as soon as they had walked back from church. He had said that they were going bike-riding and weren't even going to stop to have lunch first. Missy had mixed emotions. It had been some time since she had last ridden, but Alex had been so excited about the idea. She had barely enough time to change before she heard a knock at her room door.

"I just have to tie up my hair," she told him when he entered.

"I have a surprise for you downstairs," he said excitedly.

When her hair was fixed in a ponytail, she came to put her arms around his neck and smiled up at him.

"You look like a boy on Christmas morning who has discovered a huge package under the tree with his name on it."

Wrapping his arms around her, he said, "You are my big package under the tree." He sealed it with a kiss.

Afterward, she chuckled softly and said, "If you keep that

up, we won't be going anywhere."

He was passing his fingers through the long, brown hair that hung in long, thick, wavy strands down her back.

"Don't tempt me," he murmured.

She gave him one more quick kiss. "Besides, you never know when Zoe will pop in."

"Where is she anyway?"

"Probably gone to lunch like most normal people around here," she responded.

"What can I say, we're just not normal people. You ready?"

She nodded and went to get her windbreaker jacket.

Outside he led her by the hand to a place where he had chained a tandem to the bike rack behind the dorm.

"Alex, it's beautiful! Yellow is my favorite color too," Missy exclaimed. "A bicycle built for two. That's clever. But where is your other bike? Didn't you say that you were bringing it back with you this spring?"

"I traded it in for this. I got this one for us, Missy. See, it has a girl's seat in back and one for a guy in front. Special order. I'll drive. It took months to get it from the factory. Isn't it great?"

She gave him a hug. "I don't know what to say, sweetheart."

"Let's go," he suggested.

Alex was proud of his new fifteen-speed tandem. It could be a great way for them to travel as well as for recreation and exercise. Balance was the key to successful operation. It was not long before they were cooperating and coordinating together.

"Having fun?" he shouted over his shoulder.

"Yes, I love it," she shouted back.

Alex had turned into the fairgrounds on the dirt road. Missy caught her breath when Alex steered off the road to ride in an open expanse of grassy field to their left.

Suddenly, Alex let out a loud, shrill shriek. His hands

released the handle bars, and his feet flew off the pedals. Missy tried to balance the bike with her feet on the ground, but it was impossible. The bike lurched and twisted as Alex's body jerked violently, and his limbs flailed wildly in any direction. Both bodies were thrust to the ground with the bike falling on top of them.

Ignoring the stinging bruises, Missy got to her feet quickly, went to grasp both handlebars, and lifted the bike from Alex's still jerking body. She lay the tandem on its opposite side and dragged it back, away from the area where Alex was experiencing his epileptic seizure.

Why wouldn't he tell me? she wondered.

Time weighed heavily upon her while she waited for his convulsive seizure to end. Finally, his body lay limp—a startling contrast to the uncontrollable convulsive spasms of moments ago.

Missy knelt beside him and put a gentle hand on his chest. His breathing was shallow but steady. She unbuttoned the top two buttons of his cotton shirt to allow for freedom of movement. When she withdrew her hand, it slid over a lump in his breast pocket.

He must have forgotten to take his medication, she now realized.

With both hands, she rolled his body over onto one side. Retrieving his jacket from the ground, she stood to shake it and then rolled it into a makeshift pillow. With it she elevated his head so that he wouldn't choke on his own saliva. Drooling was possible with the loss of other bodily functions in this state. Missy covered him with her jacket and sat down to wait, knowing that he would now sleep for a time.

When aroused from her thoughts by a soft moan, Missy opened her eyes. She leaned forward to help Alex sit up.

In a calm, matter-of-fact voice, she told him, "You had a convulsive seizure, Alex. You are all right now."

Alex sighed. "Well, now you know my secret. I just couldn't find the courage to tell you that I have epilepsy."

"I understand, love."

"What?"

"Alex, I already knew you have epilepsy."

"How could you know?"

"The night Dr. Francis almost ran us down with her car, you had a mild seizure. I have seen seizures before."

"How can you say you understand?" He pulled his arms free of her grasp. "You certainly don't have to live with the fear of your body suddenly spasming out of control." He turned his head to look at the contorted frame of the broken tandem lying in the grass. "I don't even remember what happens, Missy. When people find out that I have seizures, they shun me like a dreaded disease."

"Maybe not in the same way, but I know fear too, Alex. I can never be really sure of what I see or hear. People who don't understand usually ignore me because they don't want to bother. Alex, our physical limitations and weaknesses make us rely more on God's strength. Remember Paul's second letter to the Corinthian church, in chapter 12, when Jesus tells him in verse 9, 'My grace is sufficient for you for My power is perfected in weakness.' Then in verse 10, Paul says, 'When I am weak then I am strong.'"

Alex sighed and shook his head. "I never understood that verse."

"Alex, I love you just the way you are."

"Don't you preach to me, Missy." His tone was still bitter and hostile. "You don't know my frustrations. I've read that scripture over and over again, but it still doesn't help. You don't love me, Missy. It's pity you feel, not love."

She shook her head in disbelief, but her protest went unheeded.

He stood. "Let's go. We'll have to walk the bike back to my dorm, and I'll have my dad pick it up. Have to call the doctor too. Come on, let's get it over with."

"Alex, can it be fixed?" she asked meekly.

"Who cares," he answered curtly and fell silent while they took to the task at hand.

While she walked back to her dorm alone, Missy began to cry. She knew it was possible for a distorted idea to linger following a seizure, sometimes for weeks. Alex would need time to get over it. He would see the truth of her love in time, she hoped.

17

The Heart of the Matter

Missy did not see Alex again until the next Christian fellowship group meeting. He was sincere and pleasant as he led the proceedings. However, when he walked within the circle of chairs, he avoided the area where Missy was sitting. Following the meeting, he did make a brief statement to her, though.

"You don't have to help me with the chairs anymore, Missy. I would rather do it alone from now on." He turned to begin work.

"But, Alex, I . . . I enjoy helping you. W–we are . . . are still engaged, aren't we?" she stammered, dreading rejection.

"Oh, no. Don't kid yourself, Missy. I told you the other day. It's over between us. You don't understand? Well, I'll spell it out for you. O–v–e–r. Excuse me, I'm busy."

Missy walked quickly out into the hall, carrying the pieces of her broken heart. She hugged her Bible to her chest as she walked outside.

"Why, Lord?" The sobs did not ease the knifing pain that was twisting into her heart.

Several days passed before Missy could bring herself to talk to anyone about her feelings. One evening she and Zoe were attempting to study in their room. Missy sighed as she looked across at her friend who was sitting at the other desk.

"Zoe, it hurts so bad. I don't know what to do."

Zoe looked up. "Alex was pretty rude to you the other night. He didn't have to say it so loudly that everyone else could hear it. Now you know what I have been feeling about my . . . *mother.*" The word stuck in her throat. "Don't you feel angry at Alex for abandoning you?"

"Angry? No. I still love him, Zo. That's what hurts."

Zoe shook her head. "How can you be so forgiving?"

"I can't by myself, Zo. It's Jesus in me. See, He forgives us of all our sins—past, present, and future—when we put our trust in Him. He has already forgiven me as long as I am faithful to confess my sin. I don't have the right to withhold forgiveness from someone else."

"Hmp. I never looked at it that way. What was that about confessing your sin and being forgiven?" Zoe pulled her new study Bible from the bottom of her stack of books.

"It's found in 1 John 1:9. If we confess our sins with a sorrowful heart, He will forgive it and remove it from us." Missy paraphrased the reference.

Zoe looked at the contents page to find the right book in her Bible. "And sin is doing your own thing without praying to God about it?" Zoe asked while she flipped the pages.

Her paraphrase brought a smile to Missy's face. "I love your modern interpretations, Zo. Yes, that's it. *That's it!*" She leaned forward excitedly. "The letter, 1 John, gave me an idea. I'll write encouraging notes to Alex as he did for me." Her right hand touched the knob of the bottom drawer of her desk, although she didn't open it. Missy then pulled her own large-print Bible from the top of her book stack while her mind raced for the appropriate reference. "Thanks, Zo."

Zoe appeared to be studying her Bible and lost in thought.

Alex looked up from his book when Art entered their room one afternoon. Art handed him a white stamped envelope.

"Your mail."

"Thanks, Art."

Alex opened the envelope and sighed when he read the enclosed note to himself. It said simply that perfect love casts out fear. It was signed, "Truthfully, Melissa."

"Bad news?" Art asked.

"Nothing important."

Alex crushed the note in his hand and then aimed for the waste basket. Changing his mind suddenly, he opened his bottom desk drawer and tossed the paper inside then shut the drawer again.

"I'm glad you came to your senses about Miss Old Maid," Art said.

"Yeah. You were right about her after all, Art. It never would have worked." Alex leaned back in his chair and folded his arms across his chest. To himself, he said, "That's why I didn't want to tell her. I knew it would end up this way."

"Huh? Tell her what? What are you babbling about, Alex?"

Alex looked around. He was startled from his own thoughts by Art's question. Meanwhile, Art was busying himself at his own desk.

"Oh, nothing," Alex replied and then fell silent.

A few minutes later, a knock at their door revealed that there was a call for Alex on the hall pay phone.

"Man or woman?" Alex asked.

"Man." The student grinned.

Alex went to answer it.

"Your friend Art has no traffic violations," Todd Francis told him. "But there was one arrest. The charges were dropped since psychiatric treatment was initiated. I'm still working on the details."

"Todd, I'm not involved in that situation anymore. You can work with Pete Early on this if you want to. I'll alert him."

"Alex, what happened?"

"I don't want to discuss it now, Todd. Are you still in New York?"

"Yes. We'll have to get together when I get back, okay?"

"Yeah, I guess so. Goodbye, Todd. Thanks for calling."

"Right."

"Guess I'll have to go talk to Pete." Alex muttered as he hung up the phone and headed for the stairs that led to the fourth floor. As he neared Pete's room, he heard a crackling sound.

Pete must be home, his scanner's on, Alex thought while he knocked loudly.

As always, Pete greeted him cheerfully.

"Hi, Pete. I have some information for you."

Pete smiled and rubbed his hands together as he went to turn off his radio. "What's up?"

"Todd Francis, the insurance investigator for the college, is running a background check on my roommate. It has to do with the things that happened last semester, and Missy indirectly. I thought you wouldn't mind handling it with him."

"Sure, Alex, if that's what you want."

"Todd thinks that someone is targeting her deliberately because of the nasty notes she has been getting and the latest incident in the lecture hall. You know about Art's silly prejudice, and that is a place to start."

Alex stretched his long legs out from the desk chair,

crossed them at the ankles, and folded his hands behind his head.

"Also, don't forget about our errand boy, Charlie Harris. Does Todd know about him?" Pete asked.

Alex shook his head. "Not yet, he's still in New York."

Pete nodded. Then he ventured, "Alex, do you mind if I ask you what really happened between you and Missy? I thought you two were serious."

"All right, Pete, I'll tell you since you asked. Here it is. You see, she was mistaking pity for love. I have epilepsy."

"Oh. Well, that shouldn't make any difference to her. If you can accept her limitations, I think she can accept yours, Alex. She doesn't appear to be a hypocrite to me."

"You don't even understand. I knew you wouldn't. Just take my word for it, Pete. It never works out for me when the girl finds out about my handicap. It's over, and I don't want to talk about her anymore. So you just drop it, okay?"

Pete raised his hands and then dropped them. "Hey, don't bite my head off. I'm just your friend, remember?"

"Sorry, but it's a delicate subject. So you want the case?"

Pete nodded. He wanted to ask Alex which was the delicate subject—Missy or his epilepsy—but Pete held his tongue.

"By the way, Alex, if you need help getting your tandem to a bike repair shop, I can haul . . ."

"No thanks, Pete," Alex interrupted. "My dad is going to pick it up when he brings me home for spring break, that long weekend. I already called him about it. The bike was insured anyway."

Pete nodded again. "I guess a lot of people will be gone then with Friday and Monday off. Not a lot of holidays around here."

"Yeah, but we finish early, in May, which is nice. I'm

suddenly looking forward to finishing this semester ASAP."

"Anything else I can't help you with, Alex?"

Alex thought for a minute, ignoring the remark. "There is that play of Missy's that the group is working on for the week of final exams. How'd you like to direct it, or find someone else?"

Pete sighed. "I'll see what I can do. Alex, look, I didn't mean to be nosy, but I am your friend, and I do care about you."

"Thanks, Pete. I'll see you later. I've got a class." Alex rose to leave, turning away quickly from Pete's gaze.

Even in church, Alex avoided sitting anywhere near the front because Missy always sat there. During the next week, he got another note in the mail from her. This one quoted from 1 Corinthians 13:13: "But now abide faith, hope, love, these three, but the greatest of these is love." Then the note continued, "I am still clinging to hope for us, Alex. I still love you no matter what. Hopefully, Melissa."

The note kindled his anger like fuel added to a fire, and he again crumpled the paper and threw it in his bottom drawer.

When Sue came to tell Missy that Alex was on the hall phone for her, Missy darted out the door of her room and raced toward it.

"Yes, Alex?" she spoke breathlessly into it.

The words he hurled at her struck like a blow from an iron fist.

"Stop playing mind games with me, Melissa. I've had enough of your coy deceptions. You better stop sending me notes!" He deliberately slammed the receiver down.

Missy's shattered emotions were evident when she returned to the room sobbing. She slammed the door behind her upon entering. Zoe came to put her arms around her friend for comfort, but there was no comforting her. Finally, Missy repeated what Alex had said to her.

"Was I fooling myself?" she wailed into Zoe's shoulder. Finally, she quieted enough to speak. "Zoe, it wasn't just ego. I wasn't leading him on. I truly love Alex. I can't help it."

The mailbox had become a dreaded attraction. Missy feared the hateful notes but prayed for one from Alex. One afternoon, when she checked after returning from school, she found a message from an anonymous person. She was to meet this person who had information about the notes she had been getting in the science building. The specified time was close at hand. She hurried upstairs to drop off her books.

"Zoe, I'll be back in a little while. I may have a clue."

"Where are you going?"

"Science building. I'll fill you in when I get back." Missy dropped the message on her desk and dashed out.

As Missy was walking along the corridor in the science building, checking room numbers for the correct lab, an explosion occurred. She was thrust back against the wall and overtaken by smoke and debris. She screamed, immobilized by fright.

By the time the smoke had cleared enough for her to see, campus security guards, several police officers, and other students began arriving on the scene. Two officers were carrying a lumpy object on a stretcher past her. She clapped a hand over her mouth when she realized what it was. A policeman was speaking to her.

"Miss," he repeated, "did you see anything?"

She shook her head dumbfounded. "No. I don't see well."

"She won't be of any help," Art's deep, nasal-sounding voice snapped.

"Can you identify the victim for us?" the officer asked.

Art lifted the sheet and responded. "Ya, that was my science lab partner, Charlie Harris."

"Easy, Art."

"Alex!" Missy's plea was barely heard.

"Anybody know what happened here?" an officer persisted.

"Charlie must have blown an experiment," Art said.

"Looks like," the officer agreed. "What's she doing here?" He gestured toward Missy.

"I . . . was supposed to meet . . . someone here," Missy stammered.

"Well, if it was this guy, you're too late," an officer observed.

"Alex?" Missy pleaded again.

"Art, why don't you take her back to the dorm?" Alex suggested. "Nothing to do here."

Art grunted and grabbed Missy's wrist in a death grip. He yanked her into motion to lead her out of the building.

She did not hear him mutter to himself, "If you want a job done right, ya gotta do it yourself!"

18

The Purging Fire

The spring weekend that she had been dreading finally arrived. Missy just knew that she was the only girl on the third floor and maybe in the whole dorm. The scant number of people in the dining commons for Saturday noon lunch had proved that. Zoe had gone home with Laurie for the weekend break. Missy had been planning to go home too, but she had changed her mind yesterday, knowing that she should stay to study for final exams.

Bad move, she thought as she sat down to eat she knew not what. She began to pick at her tossed salad. Sensing a presence near her, Missy looked up.

"Hi, Missy. Mind if I join you?"

She matched the voice of Pete Early with the red hair. Relief relaxed her features.

"Pete, please sit down. I didn't think anyone I knew was still left around here this weekend. How are you?"

"Still kickin' around. How are you doing?"

"No comment," she answered flatly.

"Hey, Missy. I don't know what has gotten into Alex. I tried to talk to him, and he practically chewed my head off. He did tell me that he has epilepsy. No big deal, but I guess it is to him."

"Oh, Pete, I've tried and tried to convince him that it doesn't change anything between us, but he refuses to hear."

"I think he pities himself, Missy, and he's trying to blame you for it. Hey, I'll pray for you two."

"Thanks, Pete." She sighed. "Do you know what this stuff is?"

He grinned then answered. "It's shepherd's pie, and you have a tossed salad and peaches there."

"Oh, yeah, thanks. I couldn't tell what the main course was."

"Not surprising. You're not the only one who couldn't tell."

"Pete." She hesitated a moment then ventured, "Will you do me a favor? I wrote Alex one last note. Will you slip it under his door so he'll get it when he comes back?"

While nodding, Pete took the envelope from her. "Sure. He went home for the weekend. I can slip it in for you. I think Art is still here."

The envelope was sealed and had "Alex Marcus" typed on the outside of it. After lunch, Pete went directly to Alex's room to deliver the note. He had scrawled under the name, "Special Delivery via Pete the Early Bird."

Pete was about to bend down to slide it under the door when the door opened and Art stepped out carrying a duffle bag.

"What brings you here, Pete?" Art asked cheerfully.

"I was just going to deliver this note for Alex. Could I drop it on his desk before you leave?"

Art nodded, and Pete stepped inside to plant the note.

"Where are you off to, Art?" Pete stepped back out into the hall so that Art could lock his door.

"I'm going to finish a game." At Pete's inquisitive look, Art added, "I'm going to kill the old maid."

Pete chuckled to himself as he headed toward the stairs.

Taking a break from trying to study, Missy got up to go fill the teapot in the bathroom. She started to close the door behind her as she left the room but changed her mind and left it open. No one was there anyway.

Seeing Missy bent over the sink with her teapot, the figure in the protective suit slid quietly out of the utility closet and moved swiftly but silently down the hall toward Missy's room. He was carrying a rope in one hand. As he strode into Missy's room through the opened door, he chuckled at her ignorance. He wouldn't even need the master key that he had taken from Joe's janitorial office in the lobby. Once inside, the uniformed figure squeezed himself into Zoe's closet to wait.

Missy returned with the pot of water, closed the room door behind her, then sat down at her desk. Taking out the box of tea bags, she held it close to her face, trying to decide which flavor she wanted.

"Peppermint," she said out loud.

Zoe likes peppermint, she remembered. *That should be a nice, neutral choice.* She put the bag in her cup and replaced the box. *Alex didn't like peppermint, did he? Stop it, brain!* She chided her thoughts. The pot of hot water began to rumble, so she unplugged it quickly. Surprisingly, she poured the hot water without spilling it this time. Still feeling chilly after sipping her tea, Missy decided to get a sweater from her closet.

After closing the closet door, she glanced in the mirror as she passed the bureau. When a large blot of color in the mirror caught her eye, she leaned closer over the bureau to look at it. Her mouth opened in fear, and she turned to face, in reality, the apparition she had seen in her dreams several months before. Before she could let out a scream, Missy was swept off her feet and flung onto her bed like a sack of grain. The force of her landing caused Missy to bounce and hit her head on the cement wall on the back side of her bed. Stunned by the pain from the blow and the quick movement of her newfound assailant, Missy lay still.

"This time we're going to finish it right, Clarissa."

The voice of the figure towering over her had a deep, unmistakable nasal sound. She should know that voice. Her body was rolled roughly onto its side and thrust into the hard coldness of the wall again. The second blow to her forehead sent another dizzying wave of pain through her. Smooth gloved fingers grasped her wrists, slapping them together behind her back, then wrapped something tightly around them. Missy drifted in and out of a white haze with a dull hum ringing in her ears. She wore no hearing aids, so it couldn't be her batteries going dead. That deep, nasal-sounding voice was mumbling something from far away. Her mind screamed rape, startling Missy back to consciousness with a stab of realism. Missy forced herself to roll onto her back. She felt something warm running into her left eye, but she couldn't find her hands to wipe it. She tried to lift her legs, but they were much too heavy. The specter was no longer looming above her. She was alone again. Blackness threatened to engulf her in a wave of intense heat. It didn't matter. Nothing really mattered now. Alex was gone . . .

The tall uniformed figure closed and locked the dorm room door and sprinted down the quiet hallway to enter the utility closet again. He removed the head gear and unzipped the uniform. He quickly stepped out of it and stuffed the items back into the duffel bag. Leaving the closet, he took long, easy strides toward the exit door leading to the staircase. Passing her room again, he reminded himself that he now had about three and a half minutes before the timer would explode the bomb to start the purging fire that would rid him of the haunting evil nightmares forever.

19

Art Smart

It was close to midafternoon when Alex returned to his room on Saturday. After talking to his dad, he had decided to return early to talk to Melissa. He had promised his dad that he would try to keep an open mind.

"Art, you here?"

He shrugged his shoulders when there was no answer. He bounced his suitcase on his bed and went to pick up the envelope he had seen on his desk. Alex grinned, seeing Pete's handwritten signature below the typing. Maybe it wasn't from her after all. Tearing it open, he sat down to read it. He breathed a sigh when he read her quote of the second stanza of Missy's play:

When it hurts too much to say, "I love you,"
When it hurts too much to say, "I forgive,"
When it hurts too much to cry, "I still care,"
Give it to Jesus.

She had omitted the last part of the last line, he noted,

probably deliberately to emphasize her point to him. Under the typed quote, she had handwritten, "Over please." For a moment, he held the paper in one hand, rubbing his fingers over it, trying to resist the anger and temptation to crumple it. Finally giving in to his promise, he flipped the paper and read the reverse side.

"Oh, wow."

He folded his arms and sat back in his chair, reciting the words to 1 Corinthians 13:7 over in his mind. He shook his head. Uncrossing his arms, he slowly opened his bottom drawer to retrieve the crushed notes that he had carelessly tossed inside. After reading them with a softer heart, Alex decided to go talk with his friend Pete.

"Alex, I thought you went home for the weekend."

Alex nodded. "Dad and I had a long talk, and I decided to come back. Pete, did you know what was in that note you delivered?"

Pete held up a hand and shook his head. "It was sealed when she gave it to me at lunch. Alex, the lady still loves you. What can I say?"

"Here. Read this." Alex held out the recent note. "I don't deserve her." He slumped down into a nearby chair.

"Now you're making sense, Alex. It's about time. By the way, I have some more information about Art I think you should know."

After Pete had filled him in on Art's background, Alex asked if Pete had seen him lately.

"Yup. When I delivered the note earlier," Pete answered. "In fact, he said he was on his way out to finish some game he was playing."

"Game? What kind of game?"

"He said he was going to kill the old maid. Those were his exact words," Pete recalled.

Alex stood and started for the door. "Pete, let's go!" His voice was edged with urgency. "You call the police. I think he is going after Missy."

When Art pushed through the exit door in Falcon Hall and started down the stairs, Alex appeared on the landing below.

"Alex, where are you going?" Art stood motionless, gripping his bag.

"What have you done to Melissa? It's over, Art. I know all about you."

A slow chuckle erupted from Art's throat. "Don't worry, buddy. I've already eliminated the old maid, and I have the key too."

The fire alarm began to buzz its deep cry.

Like a cornered cat, Art leaped toward Alex. Both men tumbled and rolled down the steps to the next landing below. When they had stopped rolling, Art came out on top. Seizing the opportunity, he banged Alex's head hard against the floor several times. Then Art stood, intending to retreat, but Alex caught his foot, forcing him to fall. This time they both scrambled to their feet. Both fought skillfully and forcefully. Seconds crawled by. While trying to ignore the blows to his already stinging face, Alex jabbed hard into Art's slender midsection. Pain forced Art to double forward. This afforded Alex the opportunity to strike a decisive blow to the back of Art's neck. The tall, gaunt figure collapsed in an unconscious heap on the linoleum. Alex rolled the unconscious man over onto his back to search his pockets for the dorm room key. He found it in a shirt pocket along with some yellow cellophane butterscotch candy wrappers.

Seeing Pete and Todd approaching hurriedly from below, Alex yelled to them over the persistent noise of the fire alarm to take care of Art who was, indeed, the guilty party.

Oh, Lord, don't let me be too late, he prayed to himself. Alex took the steps three at a time. Finally, he was unlocking the door to Missy's room.

Intense heat met him at the door, which opened with a bang. Stepping back, Alex removed the fire extinguisher from its wall compartment and entered the room again. He called to her, but there was no answer. Swiftly, Alex attacked the flames with his weapon. After he had extinguished the blaze, he kicked aside the debris on the floor. He went to pick up Missy's unconscious body, with hands and ankles still bound, and carry her downstairs to the ambulance, which would take her to the Iandale Hospital for treatment.

After giving his statement to the police, Alex walked up Center Street to the hospital. He learned from the doctor on duty that Missy's wounds were superficial. But since she had a mild concussion, she would be kept overnight for observation. He would be allowed to visit and could pick her up the next morning. She had been settled into a semiprivate room but was presently its only occupant. After being cleaned and bandaged, she had already been given medication to help her sleep, the doctor had explained.

Alex pulled the chair close beside her bed. He sat down to wait, hoping she would awaken for a few minutes. She wore a white square patch above her left eye, and her face revealed some red scrape marks. Her wrists were bandaged too. His head throbbed as his own bruises screamed for attention. He knew that she had still been unconscious when placed here because she would have tried to insist that the intravenous needle be placed in her right hand instead of her left.

How could anyone cause her such violent malicious harm? he wondered.

It was unthinkable to subject this compassionate woman to

such physical abuse. Alex began to pray silently.

The thought came easily to his mind, gently, but it took shape with the impact of an explosion. Hadn't he subjected her to the same kind of emotional abuse?

"Lord Jesus, please forgive me." His whispered repentance trembled on his lips.

He rested his elbows on the coarse sheet and gently covered his face with his hands, trying to shut out the memories. Alex remembered how he had lashed out at Missy when he had experienced his last seizure. The coldness with which he had avoided her feelings of shock at the awful accident scene in the science building now intensified his headache. He had broken their marital engagement when he thought that she was pitying him. All the while he had actually been putting his own self-pity and embarrassment off onto her shoulders. Now he realized his pride had been blinding him to the real truth behind his actions.

As he crossed his arms on the bedsheet, he whispered, "Lord, I need your strength in my weakness. Forgive me."

Leaning his head carefully onto his arms, he began to weep openly.

20

A Future Inkling

The dull ringing in her ears gave way to sighing as the dizziness carried Melissa from the blackness back to reality. Then the sound seemed more like soft sobbing. A quiet *mph* escaped her lips as she opened her eyes and blinked several times. Recognition dawned as the blond head lifted to look at her.

"Alex!" Her voice was an incredulous whisper as she watched the blond head lift from her bedside. Then she added, "Alex! I must be dreaming!"

"Missy." His voice was also trembling. He squeezed his eyes shut then rubbed them quickly.

A flame of hope kindled as his warm hand closed over hers. "Alex, where . . . How did you know? I had the strangest dream." Her gaze focused on the sound of his voice.

His words spilled out in an unsteady flow. "You're all right now, darling. It wasn't a dream."

She had heard the endearment. "Alex, are you all right?"

"Am I all right?" He was lifting her free hand in both of his.

His warm breath tickled her hand as he chuckled softly against it. His lips brushed a kiss against her palm. "Missy, can you ever forgive me?"

"What?" she asked simply.

"For hurting you needlessly." He touched her hand to his tearstained and swollen cheek. "I love you, Missy. I really do love you."

The bed sighed and creaked as she began to sit up and was caught in his arms. Their lips again sealed their renewed commitment to each other. He held her close and felt her body relax in his embrace. She lifted one hand to gently touch his bruises and swollen eye. His lips silenced her question.

Then he spoke softly but clearly, "I'll explain later. How do you feel, darling?"

"Dizzy, headache, but I love you."

He was easing her back onto the pillow.

"Alex, don't go."

"Sh. I'm right here."

She held weakly to his reassuring hand. When he felt her grip loosen, he rose. Her eyes had closed in sleep. Moments later, he left for the night.

In the morning, Alex stopped by the hospital cafeteria to buy some pastries and several cartons of milk before going to Missy's room. When he arrived early, she was already dressed and ready to leave. The floor nurse protested the early hour, but Alex's gentle persuasion finally convinced her to allow it. She led them to the exit door.

They walked together, each with an arm around the other's waist. She squeezed his side when he started to cross Center Street. She knew the college was on the same side as the hospital and there was no need to cross the wide street. He glanced sideways at her as they stepped up onto the opposite curb and turned right.

"Don't worry, honey. I know where we are going. Does that bump on your head hurt?" He eyed the bandage.

"It is kinda stiff and sore," she admitted.

"Looks as if you'll have a good-sized egg there."

"And what about you?" she asked. "Where are you taking me anyway?"

"I'm all right," he replied. "I thought we would rest in the park before walking all the way back to the dining commons in one trip. I brought along some goodies." He saw her surprised look when he held up the bag he had been carrying. Again he asked her, "How do you feel?"

"Stiff and sore and hungry, now that you mentioned it. Alex, I can't seem to remember what happened yesterday very well. It seems as if I dreamed it . . . But I couldn't have because you are here with me."

The park was in his sight now.

"We're almost there, darling. We can sit and rest and talk."

Only he knew that this was the reason for taking her on this route. He felt that he needed time alone with her to help put the pieces together for her own sake and peace of mind. Finally, they were seated on a park bench, sharing pastries and milk.

Missy looked up suddenly. "Alex, did you take your medication this morning?"

Smiling now at her compassion, he reached into his shirt pocket for the pill bottle.

"I'll take it right now."

When he had done so, he finished a carton of milk and put the empty container in the bag.

"Usually, I take it in the bathroom when I go back for seconds at meals. I didn't want to be questioned about my . . . about having epilepsy. Since I don't like taking it in front of people, it's a habit I've developed to remind me to take it regularly. That's three times a day. The day I had that seizure, when we went bike-riding, I had forgotten to take it. We never ate lunch that day."

She nodded knowingly. Then, desiring to change the subject, she remembered, "Did you get my note? I had given it to Pete."

Gazing into her eyes, he repeated it partially. "Love keeps no record of wrongs, and when it hurts too much, give it to Jesus."

Missy reached out to hug him. "Alexander Marcus, I love you, no matter what."

Alex carefully lifted his head from the soft fragrance of her recently washed hair and spoke softly but clearly near her ear. "In that case, Melissa Sanders, for real and forever, will you marry me?"

Her breathless affirmation was lost in their kisses.

"Missy," he murmured while still holding her close. "Missy, now that we have straightened out tomorrow, I need to discuss yesterday with you."

Alex and Missy were inseparable for the remainder of that day. When they returned to the dorm after lunch, Missy walked toward the sofa in the lobby.

"Alex, I have to sit down before I climb those stairs again. I don't understand why I am so sore and tired. We just spent the morning in church."

He sat down beside her. "Your body isn't used to rough treatment. Do you remember what happened now, honey?"

"I know we've talked about it, but no, not very clearly. It still seems like a nightmare, Alex." Missy grasped his arm as a flash of memory surfaced. "I saw the ghost from my dream. The tall uniformed figure who was in my room was from a nightmare I had a few months ago. That voice was familiar too. I should know it. Now I know how Zoe felt when her nightmare came true. It's pretty scary."

He pulled his arm free of her grasp to hug her. "No more nightmares."

"What happened to you two?"

A familiar voice startled them apart.

Missy smiled and then greeted her roommate. "Hi, Zo. You could say we had a banged-up weekend."

"Not funny." Zoe turned her bewildered look on Alex. Looking from his black eye and swollen face to Missy's white bandage and red scrapes, she asked, "Did you two have it out?"

Both Alex and Missy laughed heartily.

"No, no. We finally got it right."

Alex explained briefly how he had rescued Missy from Art, who had been the arsonist all along. He told her that Art had enlisted the aid of Charlie Harris to help make the homemade explosive devices.

"Alex, he said something like that to me." Missy thought for a moment to remember. "Art said, 'This time we're going to finish it right, Clarissa.' Yes, that's how he put it."

"Have you ever heard that name before, Missy?" Alex prompted.

After thinking a moment, she remembered. "Yes, it was on the envelope with my Valentine card." Missy looked at Alex. "It was the card that came with the burned rose. It was for Clarissa Sanders. I think I may still have it." She stood.

Alex and Zoe followed her upstairs.

"Why is that name so important?" Zoe asked.

Alex waited for Zoe to shut the door behind them and then sat down to explain.

"Apparently, Art knew a girl in high school named Clarissa

Mandez who was totally blind. He told me that he had asked her out but she refused him. I guess he dwelled on this and developed a distorted hatred for her and all other people who have disabilities in the world in general. It seems to me that he must have envied the attention she got. Art said that she died in a fire in the school gym during their senior year. He didn't tell me that he had set the fire. Either he relived his distorted notion and mistook Melissa for Clarissa, or he transferred his delusion to her along with his hatred."

"Alex, I don't understand." Zoe wiggled uncomfortably on her desk chair to face him. "How could anyone develop such hatred? I mean, he tried to kill over envy?"

"'Where envy and jealousy are, there is confusion, disorder, and evil.' Alex paraphrased from the book of James 3:16. "In other words, evil begets evil, and good yields eternal blessings."

"Remember how Art kept turning the verses around? He was trying to justify his actions for his own purpose, probably to ease his conscience. He was using the Bible, not listening to it," Missy added thoughtfully.

Zoe nodded slowly. "I think I know what you mean."

After a silent pause, she asked, "What about Joe's house fire? Surely that wasn't related to our troubles on campus?"

Alex thought for a moment. Then he answered, "I think it was. Come to think of it. I had told Art that Missy was there that night. He must have been targeting her all along. She was present whenever something happened."

"But what about the bomb threats?" Zoe persisted.

"It was a totally unrelated chain of events, but Art used it to his advantage. The police will probably want these notes, especially that card and envelope for Clarissa Sanders, Missy," Alex concluded.

She nodded. "I know. I'm going there for questioning after

school tomorrow. I'll take all of them—except the ones from Alex." She smiled proudly, holding them up.

She separated them from the others and put his back in the drawer. The others went into her purse.

"What will happen to Art now, Alex? Will he go to jail?"

Alex shrugged his shoulders. "I don't know. There will be a trial, I expect."

"Maybe he'll be put in a hospital for psychiatric treatment," Zoe suggested. "It still seems hard to believe. But looking at you two . . ." Zoe shook her head.

"No more pain," Alex said quietly.

"What?" Missy asked. "I didn't hear."

"Never mind," Alex amended. "God's strength is sufficient."

Missy smiled.

"I will need God's strength," Zoe said thoughtfully.

Missy agreed, "We all do."

On the following afternoon, when Missy arrived at the police station, she found Alex, Todd, and Pete already there. After she had given her statement and handed over her evidence, they left with her. Once outside, Pete handed her a newspaper.

Arsonist Arrested!

The boldfaced headline of the *Landale Inkling* stared at her. She nodded, smiled, then handed it back to Pete.

"Good news," Pete said. "Art confessed to everything. He even admitted to starting the fire in the basement of the Student Union building where the coffee shop and bookstore are located. He should get help now."

"I have more good news," Todd announced. "I finally got confirmation from the college she's attending. Clarissa Mandez is alive and doing quite well, academically speaking."

Missy gasped, betraying her surprise and joy.

"Then she didn't die in the school fire as Art thought," Alex concluded. "Wow!" '

Todd continued, "She apparently spent enough time in the hospital afterward to lose a year of school, though. Information doesn't come easy sometimes. Well, I'll see you chaps later. I'm looking forward to the play."

After Todd had gone, Pete said, "Too bad about Charlie."

As they walked, Alex nodded and put a hand on his friend's shoulder for a moment. Then he said. "Yeah, I know, but he shouldn't have been trying to construct bombs in the science lab anyway."

"It still seems hard to believe," Missy commented.

"Let's stop by your dorm on the way to supper, Missy. We can pick up Zoe and Laurie," Pete suggested. "I don't know if they've seen the paper yet." He grinned.

"Scoop 'em, Pete," Alex teased.

Once they had seen the article, the other girls—including Laurie's roommate, Sue—had lots of questions for them as the small group walked across campus.

"How did Art make a bomb with an alarm clock anyway?" Laurie asked.

"It probably wasn't hard for a science-minded guy. Art was a science minor even though he was going to major in psychology," Pete answered. Then he added, "I guess Charlie made some mistakes, though, when he tried.

"Ooh!" Laurie exclaimed.

"Pete, how do you manage to get the story?" Zoe asked. "I mean, did the police invite you to the questioning session or something?"

Pete shook his head and grinned. "Not exactly. It's kind of a matter of timing and persistence. You have to go after what you want and keep digging, so to speak."

Out of the corner of his eye, Alex saw Missy try to suppress a sheepish grin.

On the Saturday before final exams week began, the turnout for the Christian group's play "Nowhere to Turn" was larger than expected. Although not all were in the cast, most of the group's members had a part in the production of the play. When Missy heard more clearly than she saw, Alex performing the musical portion, her heart ached for joy. Alex sang solo accompanied only by his guitar. His voice wavered during the second stanza, but the audience thought it had been planned to add emotional emphasis to the piece.

Missy prayed silently. "Lord, you have abundantly fulfilled the desires of my heart. I do delight in your goodness." Following the presentation, the grateful group bowed to a standing ovation.

Then Alex took center stage and held up his hands for attention.

After thanking the gracious audience, he announced, "With the uncertainty of life and the finality of death, there surely would be nowhere to turn without the Living Savior. If anyone here desires to know how to receive God's free gift of eternal life through His Son, Jesus Christ, come to the front of the auditorium, and one of our group will be privileged to pray with you."

Susan, Laurie's roommate, was beside herself with tears of joy when her boyfriend, along with many others, went forward. They were going to take the step of faith for salvation and put their trust in the Living God.

Later, when the group had begun to disperse, Missy found herself in Alex's arms weeping happily.

Finally, she whispered to her fiancé, "Alex, I never dared to be this happy." She looked up. "I wish this night could last forever."

"Got it right here." Todd held up his movie camera and smiled. Then he added, "I even took some close-up shots of the audience. Ashley will be surprised, I'm sure."

"Todd, that's great!" Alex hugged Missy again.

"Wonderful performance!" Barbara added her sincere congratulations.

Zoe approached them slowly. "Dr. Francis." She held out her hand. "I am glad you came."

Barbara received it warmly. "So am I, Zoe."

"I have been meaning to talk to you." Zoe hesitated. Her grip tightened, and then Zoe let go of the other woman's hand. "I am sorry about your accident, and I'm sorry, I mean, about us. This isn't easy. I'm trying to say that I want to forgive you. Maybe we should . . . could get to know each other better . . . Mother."

Through her tears, Barbara nodded and smiled.

"Now all we need is for Alex and Missy to set the date," Pete suggested. "Do you have an official statement, Mr. Marcus?"

"How about right now?" Alex pleaded teasingly.

"It's very tempting," Missy admitted. "But I think we should wait until we finish school."

"This summer then," Alex decided.

"I mean, graduate from school," Missy corrected.

"Oh, Melissa." Alex folded his arms across his chest.

Pete said, "Well, maybe not."

A sneak peek at
the next novel,
The Snowball Effect

4
Blind Fear

Alex pointed toward the table where Clara and Tom were eating breakfast when they entered the dining room the following morning. "Let's join Clara and Tom. Oh, and here comes Sam too." Alex lifted a hand in greeting.

"So you're really gonna try it again Alex?" Tom teased.

Alex nodded and grinned faintly.

"He may surprise you today, Tom." Sam encouraged. Turning his head he asked in a softer voice, "How are you today, Clara?"

"Ready to go. I want to ski as good as Tom by the end of this vacation. You watch me."

"You can count on that." Sam promised.

"Well, when do I get to pair up with her?" Tom asked.

"Probably not until next week at the earliest. Doug is a tough taskmaster. You sighted guides will practically have to be able to ski in your sleep before he has confidence to give you a blind partner. Safety takes priority." Sam explained.

"Absolutely." Tom was quick to agree.

"Sam, do you think we could go out for another private lesson during lunch period, please?" Clara begged.

"What's this?" Tom asked.

Clara turned toward him. "Never mind, Tom. This is between Sam and me." She turned back. "Please, Sam?"

"It would be my pleasure lovely lady."

Sam's soft voice whispered tenderness and seemed oddly comforting to her troubled spirit.

Tom's chair snarled it's protest when he pushed it back to allow him to stand. "If you people will excuse me, I'm going to check my equipment before exercises. Clara, you be careful." He picked up his tray and left the table.

"Tom really cares about you doesn't he?" Missy asked Clara. This morning Missy had an affectionate attitude toward Tom's directness.

"We have been through a lot together. He knows me too well."

Sam reached over to touch her hand for a moment. "I would like to get to know you better, Clara. Your enthusiasm brings a new dimension to the sport for me."

Missy looked toward her husband and smiled.

Alex leaned back in his chair and folded his arms across his chest. He shook his head slightly and then turned it to look at Clara. He had watched her rubbing her eyes. He wondered if he should venture to ask her what was causing her such trouble to be losing sleep.

"Alex," Missy asked, "are you going to take your medicine?"

"In a minute." He uncrossed his arms to pick up his juice glass and finish it. "I'll be right back. Does anyone want anything?"

"Another raspberry tart and tea?" His wife asked. She saw him smile as he reached for her cup and leave the table.

"Clara," Sam asked, "would you like me to ask Doug if I can be your instructor? He should be assigning a permanent pairing of staff instructors to trainees today for your one to one training."

His voice sounded hopeful to Missy.

"Yes, I believe I would like that." Clara agreed.

"Great." The inflection in Sam's voice reflected his eagerness as well. He also rose to leave the table. "Excuse me, I'll go and arrange it with Doug now."

When the two young women were left alone Missy exclaimed,

"My goodness, Clara, it looks as if you have two suitors."

Clara shook her head in quick denial. "Oh, no, no. You misunderstand, Missy."

"I don't think so." Missy countered. "I didn't think any guy could be interested in me either and look what happened."

Clara giggled. It was a nice pleasant sound. "You really think so?" She asked.

"Believe it." Missy encouraged her.

"Is Alex still here?" Clara asked then.

"He went to take his medication. He'll be right back."

Clara sighed. "I wish I could sleep better. I feel so dragged out."

"Is something bothering you." Missy prompted.

"I keep having nightmares. They are very strange dreams."

"Do you want to tell me about them?" Missy asked.

"I do not know. Tom says that I should not talk about them."

"Why not?"

"Well..." Clara stopped speaking when she heard a plate being set on the table. "Alex is back?"

"Yes Clara." He responded amiably. "I brought you some fresh coffee and another pastry."

"Thank you, but I am not really hungry. I will just drink the coffee."

"Okay then, I'll take your tart if you don't mind."

Clara nodded. "I was telling Missy that nightmares keep me awake at night. I wish I could sleep better."

"You do look tired." Alex admitted.

Clara moaned a little. "I am getting a head ache too."

"Alex, let's pray." Missy suggested earnestly.

He nodded and took Missy's outstretched hand. "Clara, give us your hands. Reach out under the table and we will pray with you." Alex told her.

Clara took their hands while Alex prayed softly for God's intervention and direction on her life.

When he had finished she thanked him meekly.

"It is our privilege." Alex assured her. "God cares about all of His people no matter what circumstances they are in. I learned that one the hard way." Alex admitted.

"I think I will start over to the meeting room now." Clara stood and picked up her breakfast tray. "Thank you again Alex and Missy." She started to move slowly sliding her cane along the floor for guidance.

When she had walked away Alex turned to his bride. "How about a little encouragement before I have to leave you for the morning?"

Missy smiled and put her arms around Alex's neck. "You don't need any encouragement." She raised her face to his.

"Oh yeah?" He dipped his head to meet her kiss. "Lots." He kissed his new wife again. Alex pulled back as wood slapped against his ankle and his identification bracelet jingled. "Ow!" He exclaimed in surprise.

"Oops. Sorry Alex. What in the world is that sound?" Burt stopped just short of collision.

"It's my medical alert identification ankle bracelet." Alex told him.

"Sorry. I didn't know you were there." Burt repeated.

"That's all right." Missy answered.

"You're supposed to watch where I'm going." Burt asserted loudly. Then he continued to tap along his route with his cane.

"Guess we'd better get movin' honey." Missy said as she stood.

"Right. See you later love." Her husband answered.

They each went to their separate instruction areas.

The morning was spent becoming familiar with the ski equipment, how to check it and care for it. Again Sam and Clara came in late for lunch. Afternoon practice went as smooth as ice.

At the dance that evening the festivities began with a waltz. The newlyweds were invited to lead with the first dance. As they walked slowly onto the open floor Missy protested.

"Alex, everyone will be looking at us."

He squeezed her hand that he was holding and then faced her to encircle her back with his other hand. "Don't worry darling, it will be fine. Just concentrate on me." He smiled as the corners of her mouth turned upward slightly warming his heart. His arm gently coaxed her hand inward, against his chest where he entrapped it there. They moved slowly and gracefully, preoccupied with each other, not really concentrating on where they were going, lost to the moment. The applause captured their attention, halting their memories, calling them back to the present and ceased their descent into oneness for the time being.

Now Doug was inviting the guests and the rest of the staff to join in.

"Hey Brenda, let's show em' how it's done." Burt had stood and was waiting for a reply.

"Uh, Burt," Doug began to suggest, "why don't you try it with Marie first?" Doug kept his eyes on Marie's parents who were giving each other questioning glances.

Marie took her cue and walked over to the elder man. "Don't worry, Burt. I won't step on your toes."

He laughed and reached out to take her elbow allowing her to lead him onto the dance floor. Her parents and several other couples joined them and the Marcus's as the music resumed.

"Clara, it would be my honor to dance with you."

"Sam? But I thought you had another job in the evening?"

"I do get days, or nights, off once in a while you know." He took her hand and drew her up from the chair into an infinite warmth that she could not explain to herself.

Tom got up and walked over to a bewildered looking Brenda. "Hi, Brenda. If you would like to dance with me I promise I won't bump you into anybody. I'm Tom."

"Yes, thank you for asking me, Tom." Her smile was shy.

Sam and Clara glided smoothly around the floor like two skiers traveling a familiar path. Clara felt as if a weight had been lifted from her shoulders allowing her spirit to climb. She was breathless when the dance finished. "Sam, that was wonderful."

The next dance was a faster pace.

"Missy, how about you and me this time? Come on, what daya say?"

Missy looked at Alex and began to shake her head. "I don't know."

"How about it? Ol' Burt's a pretty good stepper even if I do say so myself." Burt persisted. "Alex won't mind this once. Right Alex?"

"I don't usually dance with strange men." Missy blurted out.

"No problem. I'm not strange." Burt countered. "How 'bout it?"

"I, I meant that I don't usually dance with guys that I don't know very well." Missy amended.

"Go ahead honey, just once." Alex urged her to go ahead and get it over with and then maybe Burt would leave her alone after that.

Missy made a face in her husband's direction and walked over to where Burt was waiting. "Okay, Burt, just this one dance."

"Great. Gotta keep up my image you know."

"Alex, I hear you need a partner?"

He turned to see Brenda shift her feet uncertainly as if she was uncomfortable. Desiring to build her confidence, he tried to make his voice as earnest as possible. "My pleasure Brenda." He reached for her hand to lead her onto the floor. Alex could see the same self conscious stiffness in Brenda's movements as he had seen in Missy's except when he held his wife. "Relax, Brenda. You are doing fine. How do you like your skiing lessons?"

"Oh. It's fun. I ski better than I dance."

"You'll get better with practice. I dance better than I ski." He told her truthfully.

"Really? I didn't think that sighted people would have any trouble."

"Skiing is a matter of balance and mine is sometimes off."

When the music finished Alex escorted Brenda back to her seat and thanked her for the dance. Then he set out to find Tom.

"You got a minute Tom? I have been meaning to have a word with you."

"Guess so." Tom walked with him out into the hallway.

"I don't mean to be too forward," Alex began, "but I am a practicing psychologist. I was wondering how much you know about Clara Mandez's past."

"Why?"

Alex hesitated in order to choose his words carefully. "I have my reasons. I will explain after you answer the question. My interest is to help her face her problems."

"Hmm." Tom pulled on his chin with the tips of his long slender fingers. It was an unconscious gesture. "So, she didn't fool you with her independent air? Well, I assume that you won't break a confidence?" Tom countered with another question.

"Of course, I wouldn't. My wife and I are completely trustworthy. You have my word on that."

"What does your wife have to do with this?"

"She is involved with Clara's past, more so than I am."

Tom released his chin to shove his right hand into the side pocket of his pants. "Well, I don't want to betray Clara's trust you understand, but she came to the University to be the research subject, not to conduct the research. She has undergone hypnotherapy as a dream research subject to alleviate nightmares that have resulted from a past tragedy."

Alex nodded. "Go on."

"She was severely burned in a fire when she was in high school and she still has recurring nightmares about it. I am a technician from the dream research lab keeping her under observation while she is on vacation. Of course, I am in constant contact with her physician back at the University." Tom did not supply the physicians name.

"Then you do know about Arthur Wills?"

Tom's eyebrows raised in a gesture of surprise. "How do you know that name?"

It was Alex's turn to explain. "He was my college roommate when I was an under graduate who tried to kill my then ex-fiancé Missy by arson. That's how we found out about his attempt on Clara. You can imagine our surprise when we literally bumped into her at the airport."

Tom's expression clearly indicated surprise. "I had no idea."

"Now you know where I am coming from." Alex summed it up. "If we can be of help to Clara in any way we will. She seems to be pretty open to talking with Missy. You know how women are."

"Mmm." Tom's hand went to his chin again and pulled. Following several moments of silence Tom finally spoke. "You said ex-fiancé. You mean you've been engaged to her twice?"

"Yeah, you could say that. It's another long story that I don't need to go into right now. It isn't relevant to the situation at hand anyway." Alex explained. "I guess I'd better go find my wife before she thinks that I've deserted her. Be glad to help, Tom."

"I will definitely keep you in mind, Alex. Count on it." Tom raised his hand in salutation as Alex walked away.

When Alex reentered the large meeting room he found his wife sitting with Clara and Sam talking together.

"Well, Alex, we were thinking of sending the rescue squad out to find you." Sam teased.

"Alex, where did you go?" Missy sounded upset.

"I saw you were busy so I took the opportunity to have a chat with Tom." He answered.

"What on earth for?" Clara asked. Concern edged her voice.

"Oh, just one professional to another." Alex sat on a chair which he had placed near his wife's. "I was curious about his work."

"He just hooks up machines and takes readings." Clara said.

"That can be interesting to another technician." Sam observed.

"Well you could have at least told me that you were going

out for awhile." Missy protested.

"Sorry honey. I didn't think you would miss me." Alex leaned closer to his wife so that she could see his face. He was smiling innocently.

"Yeah, well, don't try to make up to me."

"Clara, may I have another dance?" Sam asked. He was already on his feet in front of her as soon as the music began to play again.

Clara stood smiling happily and took his lead.

"May I have this dance, Fair Lady?"

Missy sighed at her husband's use of his affectionate term for her and stood to put her hand in his. On the dance floor she kept her outstretched hand rigid and tried to maintain a casual embrace with the other arm.

Alex leaned close and dipped his head near to her ear. Her hearing aid squealed at his nearness but he still spoke softly but clearly into it. "You were right about Clara."

"What?"

His affection toward her ear sent shivers down her spine.

"Tom knows all about Art Wills and Tom is trying to help Clara deal with her past. I was just talking to him alone. That was where I went earlier, to find Tom."

"Oh I knew it!" Missy released his hand to hug him with both arms.

He drew his head back to face her. "Does this mean that we are friends again?"

"Better than that darling." He did not miss the twinkle in her eyes. "We are lovers."

"Is it always that easy to make up?" Sam tried to sound innocent when the four of them went back to sit down again. Alex shrugged his shoulders silently and made a face causing Sam to chuckle softly.

"Where is Tom?" Clara asked.

"I think he went to make a phone call." Alex answered her.

Sam turned his attention back to Clara. "Are you having a good time, Clara? I know I am enjoying your company very much."

"Oh, yes, thank you. But it still isn't as good as skiing."

Alex grinned and then said, "Well, I don't feel that way."

"Your right of preference is fine," Sam agreed, "but you are here for skiing lessons and in that, you have no other choice."

"Mmm. Well, on that note I think we will turn in." Alex replied.

Sam and Clara seemed hardly to notice when Alex and Missy got up to leave the room.

"When will we start on steeper hills?" Clara was asking Sam.

"Each trainee works individually with his or her instructor. We go steeper when I say you are ready to go." Sam's heart warmed at her delighted smile. "Clara I have never had such an eager student."

"I love the feeling of freedom when I glide downhill. I have never known such pleasure. It is like casting all of your cares to the wind and concentrating on being care free for that moment."

"Cast all your cares upon Him." Sam quoted softly.

"What?"

"Oh, it's a quote from Scripture." Sam explained.

She grunted. "I believe but I do not read it."

"You can. There are Bibles in braille, on tape and even computer disks."

Clara shrugged her shoulders. "I just never looked into it. I have a phone number for my horoscope though. I call it every day."

"Oh no. You really believe in that silly superstition?"

"It is not silly superstition." She retorted. "It is the truth. Besides, it works."

"God's Word is the truth." Sam said. "It can set you free."

"I am free, Sam. I choose to believe in astrology and I do."

Sam sighed his disapproval.

Clara stood and stretched her white cane out in front of her. "Good night, Sam. I can find my own way upstairs. Thank you." With that said she tapped on her way.

Once on the landing upstairs she turned right to follow the short railing along counting her paces. Then she turned to cross the hallway to feel for her door number. Yes, she had stopped across from number eight. Finding it locked, she began to fish in her purse for her key. She opened the door to be greeted by a hot stuffy room. After closing the door quietly, she stood for a moment leaning against it. She barely noticed the music playing softly. *Surely, I did not leave my recorder on?* She asked herself silently. *No, I remember. It is playing the Spiritual Gifts tape. Why I know I was not even playing that one.* Bewilderment flipped her stomach into fear when she heard the crackling sound. Panic seized her. Clara turned, struggled with the door knob and finally got it open. Slamming it behind her she started across the hallway to grip the short railing. "Sam! Sam! Come quick!" Her voice was strained.

The sound of running steps matched the pounding of her heart and Sam was soon beside her now trembling body asking what was wrong.

"Fire...in my room!" She stammered.

Sam took the key from her clenched hand and went to open the door.

BONUS MATERIAL

Where Will You Turn?

(A Play—One Act, Four Scenes)

Marlene Mesot

Act 1, Scene 1

(*Present time in boss's office.*)

Mr. Thomas: (*Sitting behind his desk, holding papers in one hand and idly tapping the surface of the desk with the other.*)

(*Enter Dana UC. Dana walks to the office door and knocks.*)

Mr. Thomas: (*Looks up from papers.*) Come in.
Dana: (*From UC enters office UL.*) You wanted to see me, Mr. Thomas? (*Crosses hands one over the other in front of stomach.*)
Mr. Thomas: (*Snickers.*) Clear out your desk, Hunt. You're fired!
Dana: (*Silently expresses surprise, hesitates, then stammers.*) What... but... why?
Mr. Thomas: (*Taps papers on desk impatiently.*) Cuttin' back. (*Gestures toward the office door.*)

(*Exit Dana to walk slowly DC in dejected mood.*)

(*Enter Tony UC who walks toward Dana. They shake hands.*)

Tony: What's happening, buddy?
Dana: Can you believe it? I just got fired! Can you help me?
Tony: (*Expression changes. Shakes head.*) Tough break.

(*Exit Tony UC.*)

Dana: (*Goes to UR, a room in his house.*) Honey, I'm home.
Corey: (*Enters UR to DR.*) I don't know how much longer I can take this, Dana.
Dana: What are you talking about?
Corey: I already know you got fired.
Dana: How could you know?
Corey: Tony called. I don't know how much longer I will put up with this, Dana. (*Folds arms.*) Why don't you go take a walk or something.
Dana: Will you be here when I get back?
Corey: I really don't know, Dana.

(*Exit Dana DR.*)

Curtain

Chorus: (*Sings.*)
    When your employer sends you swiftly out the door.
    When your best friend your presence does ignore.
    When your partner says "I don't need you anymore."
    Who will you turn to?
    (*Short pause.*)
Chorus: (*Sings.*)
    Only Jesus, only Jesus,
    Can turn your life around,
    Take mixed emotions,
    And reverse the upside–down feelings—
    Take the fire from the pain,
    Only Jesus.

Act I, Scene 2

Corey: (*Opens bureau draws with anger and frustration, pulls out clothes and throws them into a suitcase, then stops, looking up. Seeing wedding photo on nearby table, sighs, slowly moves to pick it up, and shakes head.*)

Chorus: (*At the same time during Corey's actions, sings.*)
When it hurts too much to say "I love you."
When it hurts too much to say "I forgive."
When it hurts too much to cry "I still care."
Give it to Jesus, and then you'll start to live.

Corey: (*While holding photo, begins to weep quietly.*)

Chorus: (*Sings.*) Only Jesus.

Corey: (*When setting picture back onto table, knocks Bible to the floor. Stoops, picks it up, holds it face out to show front cover. Then sits, opens it, and begins turning pages.*)

Chorus: (*Continues singing.*)
Only Jesus
Can turn your life around. Take mixed emotions,
And reverse the upside-down feelings—

Take the fire from the pain.
Only Jesus.

Curtain

Act I, Scene 3

Dana: (*In boss's office sitting behind boss's desk, smiling, hands locked behind head, is pleased with self.*)

(*Knock on door.*)

Dana: Come in. (*Straightens in chair and lowers hands to desktop.*)

(*Enter Mr. Thomas DC.*)

Mr. Thomas: (*Hands folder to Dana.*) Here is the proposal I prepared for the ideas we discussed earlier. (*Begins to sit, facing Dana.*)
Dana: Oh yes. (*Glances at folder.*) Well, this won't take long.

(*Mr. Thomas rises.*)

Dana: (*Clears throat.*) The fact is (*looks defiant*), I have decided to do this one on my own, sir. (*Hands folder back to Mr. Thomas.*)
Mr. Thomas: Oh? I see. (*Turns around to leave.*) Nice to see that your success hasn't gone to your head.

(*Mr. Thomas exit DC.*)

(*Knock on door.*)

Dana: (*Glances at watch.*) Come in.

(*Enter Tony DC. Tony extends hand to Dana to shake.*)

Dana: (*Refuses hand.*) Well, Tony. Haven't seen you around for a while. What brings you around to see me?
Tony: (*Smiles nervously.*) Actually, I was hoping I could ask a favor of you, Dana.
Dana: Really?
Tony: Well, if you can't go to an old friend . . .
Dana: You dare to say that to me!
Tony: Well, we were close once.
Dana: A lot has happened since then. Get to the point. I have work to do.
Tony: (*Shakes head.*) Somehow, I thought you would understand, Dana.
Dana: (*Stands.*) Nobody helped me when I needed it, Tony. Now get to the point.
Tony: Never mind, if that's the way you are going to be. (*Turns.*) I wouldn't ask you for a job if my life depended on it. Some friend.

(*Exit Tony DC.*)

Curtain

Chorus: (*Sings.*)
    When you're on top now, and you've reached your final goal,
    When your success is a story to unfold,
    Tell me now, what will the future hold?

Where Will You Turn?

What will you turn to?
Only Jesus, only Jesus,
Can turn your life around,
Take mixed emotions,
And reverse the upside-down feelings—
Take the fire from the pain,
Only Jesus.

Act I, Scene 4.

(*Enter all cast, except Dana and Chorus, to stand around tombstone with Minister DC.*)

Minister: (*Holds Bible open.*) Though I walk through the valley of the shadow of death, I will fear no evil if thou art with me, oh, Lord. We are gathered here today to remember the passing of Dana Hunt. It was not my privilege to know this self-made business success. Life withers away all too soon for some. One may not know the decisions and opportunities lost when death intrudes unannounced. Friend, if Jesus is knocking at the door of your heart, please don't, like Dana Hunt, put off answering his call. Amen.

Chorus: (*Sings while walking to join the others on stage.*)
    Ashes to ashes,
    Dawn to dust ever so quickly.
    Where is your faith now?
    Tell me what do you believe?
    Where will you turn to?

    Only Jesus, only Jesus,
    Can turn your life around.
    Take mixed emotions,

And reverse the upside–down feelings—
Take the fire from the pain.

(Enter Dana R. Stands center stage.)

Dana: *(Sings solo.)* Only Jesus.

Curtain

About the Author

Marlene Mesot was born an only child, grandchild, and niece from Manchester, New Hampshire. She and her deceased husband, Albert, have two sons, two grandchildren, and English mastiff dogs.

She shares her heroine's disabilities of legal blindness and hearing aids use due to nerve damage at premature birth. She has loved writing since early childhood.

Marlene holds a bachelor of education degree from Keene State in Keene, New Hampshire, and a master's in Library and Information Studies from U-NC Greensboro, North Carolina.

www.ingramcontent.com/pod-product-compliance
Lightning Source LLC
LaVergne TN
LVHW010200070526
838199LV00062B/4430